Holiday Spirit

"I intend to discover your reason for jilting me, Toni," Lyonshall said.

"It has been nearly two years," she said, refusing to look at him. "Do me the—the courtesy of allowing the entire incident to remain undisturbed."

"Incident? Is that how you recall our engagement, as a meaningless *incident* in your past? Is that how you remember our lovemaking?"

LISA KLEYPAS

"One of today's leading lights in romantic fiction."
Seattle Times

Surrender

"Laura. There are some things I'd like to teach you."

Jason's hand slid to the back of her neck and tilted her face toward him.

Nervous chills ran down her spine. "Whatever you wish."

A smile pulled at the corner of his lips. "What I wish for is a kiss from my wife."

KAY
HOOPER
LISA
KLEYPAS

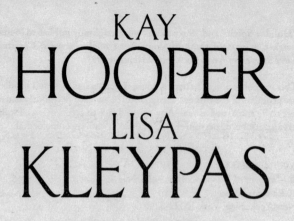

Gifts of Love

AVON BOOKS
An Imprint of HarperCollinsPublishers

"Holiday Spirit" and "Surrender" were originally published in mass market as part of the anthology *Avon Books Presents: Christmas Love Stories* by Avon Books in November 1991.

AVON BOOKS
An Imprint of HarperCollins*Publishers*
10 East 53rd Street
New York, New York 10022-5299

First Avon Books paperback printing: November 2006

Avon Trademark Reg. U.S. Pat. Off. and in Other Countries, Marca Registrada, Hecho en U.S.A.
HarperCollins® is a registered trademark of HarperCollins Publishers Inc.

Printed in the U.S.A.

10 9 8 7 6 5 4 3 2 1

Contents

Holiday Spirit

KAY HOOPER

One

True love is like ghosts,
which everybody talks about
and few have seen.

FRANÇOIS, DUC DE LA ROCHEFOUCAULD
(1613–1680)

*I*n the huge, drafty, and chilly drawing room was an intense and profound silence; the sort of silence, Antonia reflected bitterly, that her grandmother had perfected over fifty years of methodical practice. Like the icy blue eyes gazing out of the aged but still handsome face, the silence indicated extreme offense.

"I beg your pardon, Grandmother," Antonia said stiffly, her own blue eyes still as fierce as when she had spoken the offending words, but her face schooled into a mask of regret and apology. "Wingate Castle is your home, not mine; I had no right to question your choice of guests."

"Question?" The Countess of Ware's voice was measured. "I should rather have termed it an attack, Antonia."

Even more stiffly, Antonia said, "I was taken off guard, and spoke without thinking, Grandmother. Again, I beg your pardon."

Thawing ever so slightly, Lady Ware inclined her head regally. "I observe Sophia has at least seen to it your manners are not wholly wanting."

Antonia flushed, sensing a faint sarcasm. "If I lack anything with regard to social graces, it isn't Mama's fault, Grandmother, and I won't have you abusing her."

This direct statement, though it could properly be termed rude, brought a spark of approval to Lady Ware's eyes. In a milder tone, she said, "Very well, Antonia, there's no need to mount

4

a second attack against me on behalf of your mother. I have always thought Sophia a silly goose, but neither you nor anyone else can claim I do not appreciate her true worth; she has a kind heart and a generous disposition, and well I know it."

Regarding her granddaughter sternly, Lady Ware continued, "However, that is neither here nor there. I should like to know, Antonia, why you object so violently to Lyonshall's presence here. It has, after all, been nearly two years since your engagement ended, and I daresay you have encountered one another countless times in London since that shameful episode."

Antonia gritted her teeth. In the eyes of her grandmother—and, indeed, in the eyes of society—Antonia's jilting of the Duke of Lyonshall had most certainly been a shameful, and inexplicable, action. Even her mother had no idea what had gone wrong; Lady Sophia had suffered most dreadfully from the ensuing gossip, and had nearly swooned when, some months later, she had been forced to greet the duke in public.

As for herself, Antonia had encountered him at a number of the *ton* parties; she had even danced with him at Almack's at the beginning of the present Season. It was, after all, vital to maintain an appearance of cool politeness. Nothing so offended the sensibilities as a private disagreement paraded before the gawking eyes of the public; Antonia might have committed a social solecism, but she was not lost to all sense of propriety.

"I have encountered the duke," she replied in measured tones, "and I expect to encounter him again since we are often invited to the same parties. But you must see, Grandmother, that for him to be invited to my family's home for the Christmas holidays will give rise to just the sort of gossip I have been at some pains to silence. Furthermore, I don't understand why you would put me in such a position. Nor do I understand why you have chosen to house both the duke and myself in the South wing— alone."

Lady Ware offered her a frosty smile. "Since it has been recently renovated after being closed off for fifty years, the South wing is the most comfortable section of the castle, Antonia, with apartments far grander than any of the rest—

even my own rooms. Are you complaining of your accommodations?"

For the first time, Antonia had the uneasy suspicion that her grandmother—famed as much for her sly machinations as for her blighting social graces—had an ulterior motive when she had arranged this little house party. But it was absurd! What could she possibly hope to accomplish?

Ignoring the question put to her, Antonia said, "Grandmother, I trust you understand that the mere idea of—of in any way reconciling with Lyonshall is profoundly distasteful to me. If you have *that* idea in your head—"

Lady Ware let out a sound which, in anyone less dignified, would have been termed a snort. "Don't be absurd, Antonia. Do you suppose I would for one moment believe that Lyonshall could bring himself to offer for you a second time after your disgraceful conduct? No man of pride and breeding could even consider such a thing."

Antonia had flushed vividly, then gone rather pale at the crushing remarks, and her lips were pressed tightly together as she met that eagle-eyed stare. "Very well, then. This is your home, and it is for you to decide where your guests shall sleep. However, Grandmother, at the risk of offending you yet again, I must request that my coach be brought around; I am returning to London immediately."

Lady Ware's expression was one of faint surprise. "You cannot have looked out a window in the past hour, child. It began to sleet and snow some time since; you would hardly set out for London in such weather. In fact, I can only hope Lyonshall has not been constrained to put up at some inferior inn on his journey here."

Angry and—if the truth were told—intensely uncomfortable at the thought of spending several days in the company of her former betrothed, Antonia could only hope he *had* been compelled by inclement weather to delay—indefinitely—his arrival at the castle. But she doubted that was so. Lyonshall not only owned the finest horseflesh in England, he was also famous for his disregard of any obstacle in his path; if he intended to reach the castle, he would do so.

Balked in her determination to avoid the situation, Antonia could only curtsy and stalk from the room, head high.

Lady Ware, left alone in the huge room and comfortable in her chair before a blazing fire, chuckled softly. She had managed to divert her granddaughter's thoughts from the—really quite improper—allocation of rooms, and that had been her primary intent. Sophia would no doubt protest the arrangement, in her fluttery way, but Lady Ware had every confidence of being able to handle *her*.

And since the "house party" consisted of only the duke, Antonia and her mother, and the countess herself, there would be no one to carry tales of what went on here back to London.

Lady Ware congratulated herself. Providing Lyonshall reached the castle, her plan should come off rather well, she thought. The weather would serve to explain why her house party was no larger; since the castle, located in the northern Welsh mountains, had seen icy weather each Christmas for decades, Lady Ware had been able to factor that into her careful scheme. She had been doubtful only of her ability to get Lyonshall here; his own country seat was his customary retreat for the holidays, and he was notoriously disinclined to respond favorably to a summons from one who, though lesser in rank, commanded considerable social power.

At her best when slyness was called for, Lady Ware had been maneuvering for months to find a way of getting the duke here. After studying the situation—and the man—she had finally hit upon an outrageous solution.

Smiling to herself as she sat in her chair, the countess reflected that a lesson in the tragedy of mistakes would do both the duke and Antonia good. In fact, if she knew Antonia—and she did, far more completely than that young lady could guess—the lesson would have a profound effect.

The stage was set. Now if only the actors who had sustained their roles for so many years would lend their support on this very important anniversary, the play could begin.

Since her father had been a younger son of the Earl of Ware, Antonia had not grown up in Wingate Castle, and she had never put much stock in the tales of its being haunted. Still, as she strode briskly along the second-floor hallway of the South wing, she admitted silently that if there was a more likely habitation for spirits of the departed, she had never seen it.

The original castle dated before the Norman conquest, though it had naturally been renovated and even rebuilt numerous times over the centuries. Along the way, its appearance and purpose had changed from fort to residence, though the Wingate family had lived and died here from the beginning.

If ghosts walked for the reasons common to folklore—tragic, untimely deaths, for instance— numerous Wingates could be said to meet the accepted criteria. The family history held more than its share of strife, illness, and violence, as well as the usual lesser troubles all families are heir to. There were records of at least half a dozen murders, two suicides, and a score of brutal accidents—all taking place either within the castle walls or on the estate grounds.

Antonia was only vaguely familiar with most of her family's long and colorful history, and had always considered Wingate Castle a moldy old relic. But one couldn't help being aware of centuries of existence, she thought, when one was surrounded by thick stone walls, velvet hangings, and long corridors lined with immense doorways.

The restoration of the South wing had returned this part of the castle to the glory of a century before, but Lady Ware had refused to modernize in any way except for the installation of steam heat. The corridor presently echoing with the sounds of Antonia's footsteps was merely chilly rather than freezing, and her bedchamber, while not exactly snug, was at least tolerably comfortable.

Antonia passed a bedchamber two doors from her own and across the hall, and noted that two of the maids were still working to ready it for the expected arrival of the duke. It had been that sight earlier, and an explanation by the maids regarding the identity of the expected guest, which had driven her to confront her grandmother. The remainder now brought a frown to her face, and the expression earned her a stern rebuke from her maid as she entered her own chambers.

"What if your face should freeze like that, milady? It's likely enough in here!"

Antonia laughed. Plimpton had been her maid since she had left the schoolroom, and despite the older woman's frequent blunt reprimands, Antonia never took offense; she often thought that even her own mother did not know her as well as Plimpton did.

"Oh, it isn't that cold in here," she said, watching as Plimpton continued to unpack her trunks. "And you can hang the silk gowns in the back of the wardrobe, for I certainly won't wear them; it *is* too cold for low-cut evening gowns."

Plimpton glanced at her mistress, shrewd eyes direct. "Lady Ware requires her guests to dress in the evenings."

Antonia lifted her chin. "I have the two velvet gowns, and the merino—"

"High-necked and dowdy, milady, and well you know it! Even Lady Ware isn't such a stickler as all that. It's the duke you want to hide yourself from, not the countess *or* the cold!"

Antonia went to her dressing table and busied herself with the already exquisite arrangement of her fiery hair, stubbornly avoiding her maid's eyes in the mirror. "You're talking nonsense, and you know it. I've met Lyonshall countless times in company, and fully expect to continue doing so in future."

Plimpton was silent for a few moments as she

went on unpacking Antonia's trunks, but it soon became obvious that she had no intention of allowing the subject to drop. With casual innocence, she said, "There must be a full dozen bedchambers on this floor, and only two of them occupied. And this wing so far from the rest of the household. Odd, how Lady Ware put you and the duke so far from the others. Alone."

Antonia was conscious of another pang of uncertainty, but pushed it resolutely aside. As her grandmother had so accurately stated, only a fool would entertain even the faintest hope that Lyonshall could be brought up to scratch a second time when the lady in question had jilted him so shamefully—and Dorothea Wingate was no fool.

Antonia responded with composure, "Lyonshall will have his valet, and I will have you; therefore, we are not alone—"

"My room, milady, is in the East wing. Another room is prepared in that wing for His Grace's valet."

Antonia was shaken by the information, but tried not to show it. She also refrained from saying instantly that she would have a cot brought into the dressing room so that her maid

14

could sleep there. She refused to appear foolishly nervous or overly concerned with her reputation. There would have been talk in London at such an improper arrangement—but this was not London. And no one in the city was likely to hear news of what went on in this isolated part of Wales.

Her voice, therefore, was a masterpiece of unconcern. "As for choosing to house the two of us in this wing, Grandmother merely wished to show off the renovations, that's all."

"Then why is Her Ladyship's chamber situated in the North wing?"

When Plimpton used the title, "Her Ladyship" always referred to Antonia's mother, Lady Sophia Wingate.

"Because Grandmother wanted someone near her own rooms," Antonia replied.

Plimpton sniffed. "I daresay. *And* I daresay Lady Ware never gave a thought to how cold your morning coffee and bathwater will be after it's been hauled up three flights of stairs and along two corridors to reach you. You are not accustomed to such vexatious service and neither, I daresay, is the duke."

It did sound a bit daunting, Antonia thought.

"We shall have to make the best of it," she said finally. "It's only for a few days, after all."

"A few days, is it? I was speaking to Mr. Tuffet just after we arrived, milady, and he's served here in the castle for nigh on to forty years; he says when winter sets on as it has today, travel is unthinkable for weeks."

The very possibility of being shut up in the castle—no matter how large it was—with the duke for weeks on end sent a shudder of nervous dread through Antonia. It was at least bearable to encounter him socially at brief intervals, when she was able to maintain her coolly pleasant mask without strain; she doubted her ability to sustain the pretense over a period of days, much less weeks. She doubted it very much.

Sooner or later, she would give herself away. Sooner or later, Richard Allerton, the Duke of Lyonshall, would realize that the woman who had jilted him was still foolishly in love with him.

Dorothea Wingate, Countess of Ware, kept Wingate Castle fully staffed, despite the fact that she was the sole occupant throughout most of the year. Other residents of such out-of-the-way and inconvenient estates as hers wondered how on earth she managed to keep servants, especially since hers tended to be a quiet life, with few visitors and fewer social events. But the truth was that Lady Ware paid her people very well. The butler, four footmen, six housemaids, three kitchen maids, and cook—as well as numerous gardeners and stable men—were amply compensated for the drawbacks of service at the castle.

The countess seldom visited London; her most recent trip had been two years previously, when Antonia's engagement had been announced. She had returned to Wingate several months later when the engagement ended, and after Antonia had refused to discuss the situation with anyone. The scandal had obviously distressed her, for Antonia knew that her grandmother had had her heart set on the match.

Her eldest son, the present Earl of Ware, was a dedicated bachelor who spent his time in London and on another of his estates outside the city, and was not much concerned with the continuance of his family line; in all likelihood, the title would perish with him. The family had dwindled over the years, and since the count-ess's younger son, Antonia's father, died leav-ing no male offspring, only Antonia remained to carry on the family line—if not the name it-self. And since the castle was not entailed, it would most probably be left to Antonia.

She wondered if that was part of her grand-mother's reason for this house party. Antonia had made no secret of her aversion to the cas-tle; it was entirely too large, too damp, too chilly, and too far from London. She did not want it. Despite her Uncle Royce's determined bachelorhood, she continued to cherish the hope that he would fall head over heels in love and start his nursery before gout or an apoplexy carried him off.

Still, it seemed possible that Lady Ware was attempting to arouse in her granddaughter's breast some flicker of feeling for the ancestral home—as well as a reminder of what she owed to her family—and had chosen this holiday visit as a first step toward that goal.

Antonia considered the situation as she dressed for dinner that evening, wrestling her distantly polite social mask into place with all her will. There was nothing she could do except keep her wits and her calm. Ignoring Plimpton's meaningful glances and mumbled remarks, she chose a heavy velvet gown in olive green. Neither the high-necked style nor the drab color was particularly flattering, which satisfied Antonia inordinately.

Lady Ware was a stickler for promptness, and dinner at the castle was served at the unfashionable hour of six; it was just after five o'clock when Antonia left her room for the long walk to the drawing room on the ground floor. She had hoped that by going down early, she could avoid a chance encounter with Lyonshall. But fate was against her.

He stepped from his room when she was still several feet away, allowing her little time to collect herself. Normally, in social situations, she saw him first across a crowded room and was granted ample opportunity for the shoring up of her defenses; now, although she had tried to prepare herself, his sudden appearance caught her off guard.

It was clearly not so with him. He bowed with the exquisite grace for which he was famed and offered his arm. His deep voice was the caressing drawl she hadn't heard from him in nearly two years.

"Toni. You're looking lovely, as always."

To say that Antonia was taken aback would have been a considerable understatement. Expecting the distant courtesy he had shown her since their engagement had ended, she had no idea how to react to his voice, the compliment, or the unsettling warmth in his gray eyes. She had a small feeling that her mouth was open, but accepted his arm automatically.

As they began walking down the long, silent corridor, she tried to collect herself, and was unable to keep from stealing glances up at him. Gifted with an old and honorable title as well as a considerable fortune, Richard Allerton had also been blessed with a tall, powerful frame set off admirably by his usual sportsman's style of dress, and a handsome face that had broken any number of thudding female hearts.

He had been called a nonesuch, his skill with horses and his athletic prowess unequaled— and uncommon in one of his rank. He was not held to be a rake, since he neither toyed with the affections of innocent young ladies nor scandalized society by openly indulging in indiscretions. He was not above being pleased in company, and could be counted on by any hostess to dance with the plainest damsel or spend half an hour charmingly entertaining even the rudest or most outspoken of matrons.

He was a paragon.

So, at any rate, Antonia had believed when she had tumbled into love with him during their first dance together. He had no need of her fortune, and had seemed interested in her views and opinions, encouraging her to share her thoughts rather than accept the usual platitudes so common among persons of their social order.

It had been a magical, dizzying experience for Antonia, being loved by him. He had treated her as a person in her own right, a woman whose mind mattered to him. Antonia had long been appalled by the "civilized" arrangements that passed for marriage; she had desired a partner, an equal with whom to share her life—and she had believed, with all her heart and soul, that Richard was that man. Until she found out otherwise.

Now, walking beside her former betrothed, her thoughts tangled and confused, she fought to raise her defenses again in the face of his changed attitude.

"This is quite a place," he said, looking around. His voice still held that drawling, caressing note, though the words were casual. "Lady Ware has done an excellent job with the renovations."

Conscious of the strength of his arm under her hand, Antonia blurted, "I hardly expected to see you here, Your Grace."

"You know very well what my name is, Toni—don't use my title," he said calmly.

Antonia caught the gleam in his gray eyes and looked hastily away. "That wouldn't be proper," she said stiffly.

"Would it not?" His free hand covered hers, the long fingers curling under her own in a strangely intimate touch. "You have called me Richard many times. You have even whispered it, as I recall. Remember that early spring ride at Lyonshall? We were caught unexpectedly in a storm, and had to take shelter in an old stable while the groom rode back for a carriage. You whispered my name then, didn't you, Toni?"

She wanted to display a dignified offense at the reminder of a scene any gentleman would have wiped from his memory, but she found herself unable to utter a word. He was stroking the sensitive hollow of her palm in a secret caress, and an achingly familiar warmth was stealing through her body.

"How delighted I was that day," he mused, a husky note entering his deep voice. "I had believed you were everything I wanted in a woman, with your excellent mind and strong spirit; that day I discovered the wonderful passion in you. You responded to me so sweetly, with none of the missish alarm or dismay our society mistakenly insists must be the response of a lady of quality to passion. I held a loving, giving woman in my arms, and thanked God I had found her."

"Stop," she managed finally, her cheeks burning as she made a useless attempt to pull her hand from his grasp. "To remind me of such a—a shameful episode—"

"If I thought you really believed that, I'd box your ears," he said, and his eyes then were a little fierce. "There is nothing shameful about the desire two people feel for one another. We were to be married—"

23

"But we were *not* married, not then and not afterward," Antonia said unsteadily, grateful to see the first flight of stairs just ahead, but painfully aware that it was still some distance to the ground floor of the castle where the presence of other people would certainly curb her companion's shocking conversation. She didn't know how much more of this she could bear.

"I am aware of that," he said evenly. "What I don't know is why we were not married afterward. You never gave me a reason, Toni. You talked a great deal of nonsense, saying that you had realized we wouldn't suit—"

"It was true!"

"Balderdash. We were together nearly every day for months, and found one another splendid company. Parties, the theater, riding, driving in the park, spending quiet evenings in your home and mine—we suited admirably, Toni."

She remained silent, staring straight ahead.

"I intend to discover your reason for jilting me. I know there *was* a reason; you are far from being so flighty as to do such a thing on a whim."

"It has been nearly two years," she said at last, refusing to look at him. "Past. Do me the—

the courtesy of allowing the entire incident to remain undisturbed."

"Incident? Is that how you recall our engagement, as a meaningless *incident* in your past? Is that how you remember our lovemaking?"

It required an enormous effort, but Antonia managed to make her voice cold. "Is that not how any mistake should be termed?"

Lyonshall did not take offense at what was, in essence, an insult, but he did frown. "So cold. So implacable. What did I do to earn that, Toni? I have wracked my brains, yet I cannot recall a single moment when we were not in harmony— except for that last morning. We had been to the theater the night before, along with a party of friends, and you seemed in excellent spirits. Then, when I came to see you the following morning as usual, you informed me that our engagement was at an end, and that you would be . . . obliged if I would send a notice to the *Gazette*. You refused to explain, beyond the obvious fiction that we didn't suit."

They were descending toward the entrance hall now, and Antonia caught a glimpse of one of the footmen, splendid and stalwart in his livery, stationed near the foot of the stairs. She had never been so relieved to see another person in her life, and a tinge of that emotion was in her voice when she replied to Lyonshall.

"You acceded to my wishes and sent the notice—why must you question me now? There is no reason to do so. It is past, Richard. Past, and best forgotten by everyone."

He lowered his voice, apparently because of the footman, but the quieter tone did not at all lessen the relentlessness of his words. "If only my pride had been bruised, I would agree with you; such shallow hurts are best put aside and forgotten. But the blow you dealt me went far deeper than pride, my sweet, and in all the months since, I have not forgotten it. This time, there will be an end to things between us. One way or another."

The endearment surprised her; it was one he had used only in passion—and it triggered a scalding rush of memories that tore at her hard-won composure. But that shock was small compared to what she felt at the clear threat of his words. Dear heaven, had he waited two years to punish her for jilting him? Or had Lady Ware's invitation presented him with an opportunity he intended to take advantage of, merely to enliven a boring holiday?

She had never believed him to be a cruel man, at least not intentionally so, and found it difficult to believe now. Had she indeed hurt him so badly? And what did he intend now? *An end to things* . . .

It was only years of practice that enabled Antonia to school her features into an expression of calm as she walked beside Lyonshall into the huge drawing room. He released her hand in order to greet her mother and grandmother, but that was no more than a brief respite since he fetched her a glass of sherry and stood near her chair as he talked with his usual charm to the two older ladies.

Any other time, Antonia would have been hard put not to laugh. Her mother, a still-pretty woman with large, startled blue eyes and fading red hair, was clearly baffled and unnerved by Lyonshall's presence, and hardly knew what to say to him. Lady Sophia had been delighted by the engagement, both for the worldly reason of her daughter's assured position in society and because she knew Antonia had loved her betrothed. But she was, by nature, a timid woman, and a situation such as this one was bound to be a strain on her nerves.

Lady Ware, on the other hand, was utterly calm and obviously pleased with herself. She was not one to charm, but she was more courteous to Lyonshall than Antonia had ever known her to be to anyone else. She seemed to have an excellent understanding with him.

"I believe we may make your holiday here a memorable one, Duke," she said at one point, her tone one of certainty rather than hope, and her use of his title a bland indication that she considered them equals despite the difference in their ranks. "Here at the castle, we observe most of the usual Christmas traditions, as well as some which are uniquely our own. Time enough to discuss those tomorrow, of course, when you have completely settled in—but I do trust you mean to be a participant rather than merely an observer?"

He inclined his head politely. "I try always to be a participant, ma'am. What is the point of a holiday if one cannot enjoy oneself, after all? I am looking forward to a very special memory of Christmas at Wingate Castle."

Antonia sipped her sherry, feeling peculiarly detached. Christmas? That *was* the reason they were all here. It was difficult to think about the usual trappings of Christmas when her mind was so filled with him. This was supposed to be an interlude of peace and good cheer, of high spirits and joy and contentment.

But all Antonia could think of were the memories Lyonshall had dragged from the locked rooms of her mind. Secret memories. To some, they might even be shameful memories.

As they seated themselves in the dining room, she looked at her mother and grandmother, wondering. What would they think if they knew about that rainy spring day? They would undoubtedly condemn her for what she had done. It was shocking enough that she had given herself to a man—even her betrothed—without the sanctity of marriage, but then to end her engagement within a week, seemingly without reason . . .

Lyonshall could have ruined her completely had he chosen, with only a few words spoken to the right people. Antonia knew he had remained silent. For his own sake, perhaps; the tale would not have ruined him, but it would have marred his excellent reputation as a gentleman. Oddly enough, it had never occurred to her then that he might do so. It occurred to her now only because of his implied threat to "end things" between them.

But surely he wouldn't . . .

"You're very quiet, my sweet."

She looked up hastily from her plate, cheeks burning; he had not troubled to lower his voice, and everyone from Tuffet and the footman serving them to her mother and grandmother had heard the endearment.

Lady Sophia all but dropped her fork, but Lady Ware, undisturbed, met her granddaughter's eyes with a faint, bland smile.

Grimly holding on to her composure, Antonia said, "I have nothing to say, Your Grace."

He was seated on her grandmother's right, with Antonia on his right, and her mother across the table. Antonia's chair was near the duke's, so near in fact that he was easily able to reach the hand lying over her napkin in her lap. Once again, his long fingers curled around hers in a familiar, secret touch.

"That, surely, is a rare event," he said with a smile so private it was like a touch.

30

Antonia couldn't reclaim her hand without an undignified—and obvious—struggle, so she was forced to remain still. But her cheeks burned even hotter when Tuffet came around to serve them. Naturally, the butler did not betray by so much as the flicker of an eyelid that he saw the clasped hands, but there was no doubt he did see.

"I have learned to rein my tongue," Antonia said with a meaning of her own. "I no longer blurt every thought aloud."

"But your thoughts are part of your charm," Lyonshall said smoothly. "I always found your plain speaking quite refreshing on the whole. Pray say whatever you wish; no one here, surely, would censure you."

Antonia gritted her teeth. Very slowly, she said, "If I were to say what I wished to say, Your Grace, I am very much afraid that both my mother and grandmother would find me sadly lacking in manners."

"I am persuaded you are wrong."

Antonia did not know what to think, and her earlier brief detachment had flown. How dared he do this to her! What did he mean by it? She could feel the warmth and weight of his hand even through her clothing, feel one of his fingers stroking her palm in a slow caress, and a tingling heat spread slowly outward from the very core of her body in a helpless response.

She wanted to be angry. She wanted that so desperately. But what she felt most was a longing too powerful to deny and almost beyond her ability to fight.

Lady Sophia, looking anxiously at her daughter's flushed cheeks and glittering eyes, and unsettled by the oddly intimate conversation going on between Antonia and the duke, rushed hastily into speech. "I do trust, Your Grace, that this wretched weather won't keep you tied by the heels here and cause you to miss very many of—of your usual pleasures! You were promised to Lady Ambersleigh's cotillion in a fortnight, were you not?"

It was such a transparent hope that the duke's unnerving presence would not be unnecessarily prolonged, it was actually rather comical. Antonia caught herself glancing at Lyonshall, and felt a spurt of reluctant amusement when she met the laughter shining in his eyes. His voice, however, was perfectly grave.

"I was, ma'am, but I sent my regrets." His gaze flickered to Lady Ware's impassive face. "Having been warned I was likely to find myself snowbound here."

Her amusement vanishing, Antonia looked at her grandmother as well. "I was not warned," she said.

"You did not ask, Antonia. Lyonshall, being a man of good sense, did ask." Placing her napkin beside her plate, the countess regarded her noble guest with a questioning lift of her brows. "Shall we ladies withdraw and leave you to enjoy your port in lonely splendor?"

He inclined his head politely. "I would prefer to forgo that custom, ma'am, with your permission."

If Antonia had cherished hopes that Lyonshall would release her when they rose from the table, those hopes were swiftly dashed. He tucked her hand in the crook of his arm and held it there as they returned to the drawing room.

He was, in short, behaving as though he and Antonia were still engaged! She did not understand what was in his mind . . .

"Play for us, Antonia," her grandmother

commanded with a nod toward the pianoforte. "I am sure Lyonshall would be delighted to turn the music for you."

Antonia considered rebelling, but at least he would be forced to release her since both her hands would be required for the task. She seated herself on the bench, and was further disturbed by the swift pang of loss she felt when he let go of her hand. Automatically, she began playing the piece already set before her, realizing too late that it was a soft, gentle love song.

Lyonshall leaned against the pianoforte, ready to turn the pages. His voice was low. "I have missed your playing, Toni."

She kept her eyes resolutely on the music, grateful only that her mother and grandmother could not overhear whatever shocking things he said while she was playing. "I am merely adequate, Your Grace, and you well know it," she said repressively.

He turned the first page for her. "If you use my title one more time, my sweet, I shall take my revenge in a manner calculated to shock your mother very much."

Antonia hit a wrong note, and felt her cheeks flaming yet again. Her practiced mask was in splinters, and her voice was much more natural—and, to her fury, helpless—when she said, "What are you trying to do to me, Richard?"

"Have you not guessed, love? I am doing my poor best to court you. Again. In fact, I have a special license, and fully intend to marry you before the new year."

It was truly remarkable, Antonia thought much later that evening as she paced her bedchamber, how the social manners drummed into one from childhood had the power to hide even the most intense emotions. The moment Lyonshall had stated his astonishing intentions, her mask had almost magically rebuilt itself, and she had actually been able to behave as though nothing out of the ordinary had happened.

She knew she had remained calm, that she had continued to play the pianoforte; she could even recall responding to several of his more casual remarks. But the wild emotions churning beneath her mask had enabled her to ignore— almost to the point of literally not hearing—the shockingly intimate things he had murmured to her under cover of the music.

Perhaps his intentions, if he had meant what he said about wishing to marry her, should have made his behavior more bearable, but for Antonia that was not so. The bitter hurt that had caused her to end their engagement was still strong in her despite the months that had passed, but even though her mind fiercely refused the very idea of marrying him, both the painful longing of her heart and the powerful desire he had rekindled whispered seductively.

It had been nearly two years. Perhaps *she* was no longer a part of his life now. Perhaps he had decided—this time—that he could be content with a wife, and feel no need for a mistress as well. Or perhaps Mrs. Dalton had grown too demanding for his taste, and he had not yet found a replacement for her. And perhaps Antonia could forgive, even forget, the terrible hurt . . .

Perhaps. Perhaps. *Perhaps.*

Antonia flung herself into a comfortable

chair by the fire, absently drawing her dressing gown tighter. The afternoon storm had continued into the night, adding its threatening chill to the cold stone walls and floors. Outside, the wind moaned fretfully, and sleet pelted the windows in a whispery cadence. The mournful sounds were a perfect accompaniment to her miserable mood. Her thoughts chased their own tails, and her feelings remained in a painful tangle.

Her mother, she knew, would never understand; that was why Antonia had never confided her reason for breaking the engagement. Her own father had kept a mistress; according to gossip, most gentlemen did. Their wives were expected to pretend that such creatures simply did not exist. But Antonia knew herself too well to believe she could be happy in such an arrangement.

Even worse, he had *lied* to her. Early in their engagement, with the frankness he had claimed to admire, she had told him that she believed both partners in a marriage should remain faithful. He had agreed with her, saying with equal bluntness that although he had enjoyed several agreeable connections in the past—he was, after all, thirty-three at that time—she was the only woman in his life, and he fully intended that that would remain true.

That he had been so clearly willing to begin their marriage with a lie had hurt even more than the thought of another woman. It had shattered her trust in him.

Even now, she didn't know why she had not told him the truth. Perhaps because she could not bear the thought that he would lie again. And although he had said in the drawing room that he meant to know the truth about their breakup, she didn't want to tell him. She was afraid he would have some ready answer, and that she would allow herself to believe it even if it was a lie.

It was nearly midnight, and though the room was reasonably comfortable with the fire blazing, she shivered a bit. She felt so alone. The thought had barely crossed her mind when she became aware of a slight stirring of the air, as if someone had passed near her, and all her senses came suddenly alive and tense. She turned her head slowly, and gasped aloud.

He stood by one of the windows looking out, frowning slightly as if the storm disturbed him.

He was wearing a dressing gown, its colors muted. He was dark, with a hawklike profile, and for an instant Antonia thought it was Lyonshall. Indeed, she very nearly cried out a sharp demand to be told what he was doing in her bedchamber.

Her bewildered anger vanished quickly, however, to be replaced by a pang of chill fear when she realized that she could clearly see the tapestry hanging just beyond him—*through his body*.

Unable to believe her own eyes, Antonia swallowed hard and managed to hold her voice steady enough to ask, "Who are you?"

He did not answer. In fact, he appeared to take no notice of her at all, as if—to him—she was not even in the room. Turning away from the window, he drew a watch from the pocket of his dressing gown and studied it, still frowning. Returning the watch to his pocket, he moved a few steps nearer to Antonia and seemed to pick up something as if from a table long since vanished. A book appeared in his hands, no more solid than he was, yet she could almost hear the whisper of pages as he leafed through them.

Antonia was still afraid, yet she was fascinated as well. She felt almost numb, her mind working with a strange clarity. Huddled in her chair, she stared at him, seeing that he did indeed resemble Lyonshall. His height and build were much the same, as was the dark hair and hawklike handsomeness. But this—man's—hair was worn long, tied at the nape of his neck with a black ribbon, and she vaguely recognized the style as that of a century past. His face was thinner, his eyes deeper-set than the duke's, and she thought he was—had been—a bit younger.

She was not dreaming; Antonia knew that. She could feel the heat of the fire and hear its crackling energy, hear the wail of the storm outside, and sense her own heart pounding rapidly. She forced herself to move, rising slowly from her chair. Again, he did not react to her presence.

"Who are you?" she repeated in a louder voice. She started when he moved suddenly, but it immediately became clear that he had no awareness of her presence. She had the eerie feeling that this was no longer her room, that it had become his. It even looked subtly different to her, as if she was the one caught between times and she could *almost* see the room as it had been in his time. Almost. But it was more of an emotional sense than an actual one, she thought; she was fixed in her own time, allowed only a kind of doorway to see into his.

For a fraction of a moment, a superstitious terror sent ice through Antonia's veins. She could not draw him into the world of the living—but what if he could pull her into the world of the dead? The fear was brief, but strong enough to leave her feeling shaken. Her rational mind reasserted itself, and she reminded herself that he had taken no notice of her; obviously, he was no danger to her.

Nevertheless, she started a bit when he dropped the book—it vanished the instant it left his hands—and consulted his watch a second time. A smile curved his lips as the watch was returned to his pocket. Then he strode toward the door.

Antonia had no intention of following him, but she found herself doing just that, as though compelled. She felt almost like a puppet, pulled along as if she had no will of her own, and that sensation, added to the appearance of the man, made the impact of these unnatural events even stronger. Fascinated, numbly frightened, inexorably drawn, she followed him.

She had a bad moment when he passed through the closed door as if it had been open, but she forced herself to turn the handle, open it for her own passage, and step out into the hall. He had paused just outside the door, and for a moment she was unaware of anything but him. Then he went on. It was easy for Antonia to see the man in the hallway; sconces placed high on the wall between each door lined the entire corridor, and they were kept burning all night.

The man was met several feet away in the hallway by a slender, very young woman, dressed in a flowing dressing gown, with a lovely, delicate face and a crop of riotous red curls worn loosely. Her huge, glowing eyes lifted to his as they met, her lips parted, and she was in his arms as if it was the one place in all the world where she belonged.

Antonia felt a vague shock when she saw the young woman, but she was uncertain as to the cause. Surely, two ghosts were no more shocking than one? No, it was something else. A sense of familiarity, perhaps, though she had no idea why that should be so, for she could not remember ever seeing a likeness of this young woman and she did not know her identity. Before she could ponder the matter further, she realized that she was not alone in observing the lovers.

Lyonshall stood in the open doorway of his room, staring just as she did. She could see him hazily through the lovers. It was a strange and eerie sight, evoking a feeling of even greater unreality within Antonia, yet she was more affected by the passionate embrace than by the ghostliness of two people long dead and buried.

Their passion for one another was so powerful Antonia could literally feel it. They kissed with the aching pleasure of two people deeply in love, their faces transformed by tenderness and desire. Their lips moved in speech that only they heard, though it was obvious they spoke words of love and need. Her arms were tight around his neck, and his held her pressed to his body. She tilted her head back as he kissed her throat, her expression filled with such sensual delight that Antonia wanted to turn her eyes from so intimate a moment.

But she could not. Just as she had felt compelled to follow the man from her room, so now she was compelled to stand there and watch. She felt caught, trapped in a spell of sensuality that tugged at all her senses. Her heart beat faster, and she felt hot, her body feverish and tense. It seemed to go on forever, but it was actually no more than a few minutes later when the couple turned with one mind and moved toward the duke's bedchamber.

Antonia felt rather dazed, but a shaken laugh escaped her when Lyonshall automatically stepped aside for them. They passed into his room. He looked after them for a moment, then reached for the handle and pulled the door closed. He strolled down the hall to Antonia.

With utter composure, he said, "I believe they would rather be alone."

"How can you be so calm?" she asked, her gaze moving between him and the closed door down the hall. Her voice was shaking, and she felt appallingly unsteady. "I knew the castle was supposed to be haunted, but it was not something in which I believed. I—I was never more shocked in my life."

He slid his hands into the pockets of his

dressing gown and smiled faintly. "Lyonshall is not so old as Wingate, but it can claim a number of centuries. And a few ghosts. In the portrait gallery, it is quite usual to see a cloaked gentleman moving about on stormy nights such as this one. I have seen him myself. In fact, he tipped his hat to me with perfect courtesy one night." He paused, then added, "I wonder why spirits choose to walk most often when the weather is uneasy. And why the hour of midnight seems to be their time."

Antonia had no answer for him, and in any case he did not wait for one.

"Well, as it appears my room will be occupied for some time to come, and since it is somewhat drafty in this hallway, I suggest we wait in your room."

Too startled to voice an instant refusal, Antonia found her arm taken in a firm grasp as she was guided back into her bedchamber. She pulled away from him, her voice even more shaky when she said, "We most certainly cannot wait here! I am astonished you would suggest anything so improper."

"Don't be missish, Toni; it hardly becomes you." He strolled over to the fireplace and stood gazing at the flames. "I have left the door open, as you see. In any case, but for our ghostly friends we are quite alone in this wing, so you need fear no scandal. By the way—do you happen to know who the lady was?"

"No."

"Undoubtedly an ancestor of yours; you are the living image of her."

That startled Antonia so much that she forgot to be affronted by his presence in her room. "I?"

Lyonshall looked at her. "Didn't you notice? The same red hair and blue eyes, of course, but there is a much stronger resemblance than mere coloring. You share the same delicacy of feature, the same large eyes and flying brows. She was less stubborn, I imagine; your jaw is sharper. And though the shape of your mouths is very alike, you have more humor than she could lay claim to, I believe."

He smiled slightly, his gaze intent on her. "As for . . . other attributes, I would say that you are far superior to your ancestor. She seemed quite frail, almost sickly. You, however, possess a magnificent body, beautifully voluptuous without an ounce of excess flesh. A body made for the passion we both know you are capable of."

Antonia felt an almost feverish heat stealing through her body once again, and silently cursed his seductive wiles. She had to regain control of this situation, before . . . before something irrevocable was said. Or done. "Please leave at once," she said stiffly.

"And where am I to go?" He raised one brow.

"There must be thirty rooms in this wing!"

"None of which have been prepared for a guest. Cold fireplaces and unaired sheets? And the furniture likely in holland covers? To say nothing of the difficulty my valet would have locating me in the morning. Would you really be so cruel as to consign me to such discomfort only to satisfy the boring notions of propriety, Toni?"

She struggled to remain calm. "There is no reason for you not to return to your room. The—the ghosts probably vanished the moment they entered; I am sure you will find them gone if—"

"No. They were moving toward the bed as I shut the door." His voice had deepened to a husky note.

Remembering the passionate kisses they

had observed, Antonia flushed. The scene had profoundly unsettled her. She couldn't seem to shake the queer sensual spell that had enveloped her as she had watched them, especially since Lyonshall seemed bent on reminding her.

She could not help but think of those two lovers blissfully together in the duke's bed, or in a ghostly bed of their own century, she surmised, and that mental image brought others with it. A quiet stable, filled with the sweet scent of new hay. His mouth on hers, arousing emotions and sensations she had never known before. The burning, throbbing longing of her body for his. The incredible, shocking pleasure of lying in his arms and discovering her own passion . . .

Antonia stood with her arms crossed beneath her breasts, and tried to push the disturbing memories from her mind. That proved impossible. She was vividly conscious of how alone they were, of the nearness of her bed and the scant covering of her nightclothes. Gradually, the eeriness of the ghostly encounter was completely overwhelmed in her mind by its sensuality, and by the flesh and blood stirrings in her body as all her senses responded to the man who stood only a few steps away.

"Sit down, Toni. We may be here a while."

"I would rather stand." She was afraid to move, certain that if she did, it would be to throw herself into his arms. Dear heaven, he had barely touched her when they had entered the room, and casually, yet her entire body longed for his touch so intensely that resisting the pull toward him was like fighting an uncontrollable force of nature. Not even her most bitter and hurt memories of what he had done could stop the building desire.

He shook his head. "So stubborn. Do you expect me to try and ravish you, is that it?"

She lifted her chin and glared at him, reaching for dignity, offended hauteur—anything to combat the clash of longing and bitterness inside her. "I *expect* you to remember you are a gentleman. Though, given your behavior today, I must admit my hopes are not high."

"Indeed? Wise of you. For I don't mean to pretend with you, my sweet. I won't play the gentleman, happily content with a light flirtation and a few chaste kisses. There is blood in my veins—and yours—not water. I refuse to behave as though my desire for you is easily tamed. It is not. I refuse to forget that you have already given yourself to me, even if you choose to ignore that fact."

"Stop."

"Why? Because a gentleman wouldn't remind you? Because society insists that if such a shocking thing were to happen, all memory of it must be wiped away? That isn't so easy, is it, Toni? To forget. Is that why you accepted none of the offers of marriage made to you this last year, because you could not forget? Or was it because your bridegroom would know he was not the first in your bed?"

"Why must you taunt me with that?" she whispered, wishing she could hate him. Anything would be better than this awful, aching need for his touch.

His hard face softened. "Not a taunt, sweet. How could I scorn such a beautiful memory? I know you felt as I did that day, that our loving was intended. You could not have given yourself to me so freely if you had believed anything else."

Antonia couldn't move or speak as he came slowly toward her. She could only wait, heart thudding, body trembling. She felt suspended, poised on the brink of something she wanted desperately even while a large part of her mind struggled not to give in.

"No, Richard," she said in a smothered voice as he reached her, suddenly very much afraid that if he touched her now she would be lost.

"Yes," he said huskily, his hands lifting slowly to frame her face. "Whatever caused you to hate me didn't change this. We both know it. You want me, Toni, as much as I want you. And if desire is all I can claim from you, I will claim that. Marriages have begun with less."

Even if she had been granted a moment to prepare herself, no barrier she might have raised could have stood against him. He took her mouth with all the passionate intensity she remembered so vividly, and her entire body responded. Her arms lifted to his neck as his went around her. She felt the hard warmth of him against her, and the strength drained from her legs in a rush.

She had forgotten how it felt . . . No, she had forgotten nothing. The heat spreading through her body, the building tension of need, the hunger that brought her out of herself until she was returning his kisses with a passion only he was able to ignite in her—all of it was achingly familiar. Just as it had been in the stable, her response to him drove everything else from her mind, until only the two of them existed in a world of sensuality.

She was barely aware of being lifted and carried a few short steps, then she felt the softness of the bed under her back. She gasped when his lips left hers, her eyes opening dazedly to stare up at his taut face. He was sitting beside her, bending over her, his hands smoothing loosened strands of her long hair away from her face. He lowered his head and kissed her so fiercely that it was like a brand of possession, and she heard the small muffled sound of pleasure that escaped her.

It was as though she had been deprived for a long time of something her body and spirit craved, and her hunger rose higher and higher, beyond her ability to control it. Just as it had been before, she didn't think of a price to be paid or the potential for pain—only the irresistible necessity of belonging to him.

His lips trailed down over her throat, then lower as his fingers untied the ribbon of her nightgown. He pressed a hot kiss in the valley between her breasts, and the vibrations of his words were an added caress.

"Tell me you want me, Toni."

It was not the demand that sent a cold rush of sanity through Antonia; it was his voice. There was something in it she had never heard before, a driven, implacable note. And when he raised his head to stare down at her, his eyes were the flat gray of a stormy sky. Angry. He was angry.

She wondered suddenly, painfully, if he really did intend to marry her. She didn't think so. She thought he wanted her physical surrender, wanted to prove to them both that she could not refuse him in this, at least.

If he wanted revenge because she had jilted him, he could hardly have chosen a better means. Because if she gave herself to him now, knowing they had no future together, in her own mind—and undoubtedly his—she would be little better than a whore.

Her throat was aching, but her voice was steady when she said, "No." Her arms around his neck fell to her sides, and she closed her eyes. "No."

He went utterly still, then she felt the bed shift as he moved away. A few moments later, the door closed quietly, and she knew she was alone.

Antonia opened her eyes and sat up slowly. Her lips were throbbing from his kisses, and her entire body felt feverish and tense. Until that moment, she had not realized just how much she still loved him. Enough so that she wanted to call out to him, or go after him. Enough so that if he had kissed her one more time, she would have been unable to say no again.

She loved him so much that she would have made herself a whore without an instant's hesitation, if only he had said he loved her.

But he had not.

That, more than anything else, caused Antonia to believe he wanted nothing from her except the satisfaction of knowing she could not resist his seduction.

The room was very quiet, growing chilly as the fire died. Antonia felt alone, and this time not even a ghost came to prove her wrong.

The following day was strange and unsettling. Antonia had not slept well; between the ghostly visitation and Lyonshall's near-seduction, she had been left in a state hardly conducive to sleep, and it had been close to dawn before she had finally managed to close her eyes. When Plimpton had awakened her only a few hours later, the lack of rest and her emotional turmoil made her feel raw and tense. She said nothing about the ghosts to her maid, and certainly nothing about the duke's midnight presence in her bedchamber, but drank her tepid morning coffee in silence.

When she went downstairs, it was with a certain trepidation, but she found only her mother in the breakfast room. Lady Sophia was not a particularly observant woman, but where her only child was concerned affection lent her acuity.

"Darling, are you feeling well?" she asked immediately, her large eyes filled with concern. "You seem tired and—and quite pale."

Antonia had already made up her mind not to mention the ghosts to her mother; Lady Sophia was of a nervous disposition, and would certainly be unable to sleep a wink if she were told that spirits roamed the castle at night.

Helping herself to toast and more coffee from the heavily laden sideboard, Antonia replied calmly. "The storm kept me awake, Mama; I am only a little tired—nothing to signify."

Lady Sophia waited until her daughter was seated at the table, then glanced around to make certain they were alone. Lowering her voice, she said in her fluttery way, "Darling, I trust you locked your door last night. I was never more shocked! I had intended to speak to your grandmother about the situation, but . . . but she looks at one in *such* a way, I felt myself quite unable to make the attempt."

It required a moment before Antonia realized her mother was referring to the arrangement of bedchambers. "I am sure you need have no fears, Mama," she said, pushing aside the memory of hot kisses. "Remember, if you please, that the duke and I agreed we wouldn't suit."

Eyeing her, Lady Sophia said, "Well, so you said at the time, but—Forgive me, Toni, but it appeared to me last night that Lyonshall was behaving with far more—more *warmth* than was at all seemly. The way he spoke to you and looked at you . . ." Blushing slightly, she added,

"My dear, though you judge yourself quite grown-up, there are some things you simply cannot know about men. Even the best of them may find themselves at the mercy of their *baser* instincts and—and for you to be all alone with the duke in that big, empty wing—and you so pretty as you are—it just seems to me—"

Rescuing her parent from the morass of her tangled sentence, Antonia said a bit dryly, "Are you referring to passion, Mama?"

"Antonia!"

She felt a pang of sad wisdom. She should have been innocent of passion, as her mother so clearly believed she was. For an unmarried young lady of twenty-one to have the knowledge Antonia possessed was shocking and should be a source of heartache. But the shame of having given herself to a man before marriage was not so dreadful to her because she had given herself in love. No matter what had happened afterward, and despite her words to Lyonshall about the "mistake," Antonia did not regret what she had done.

Quietly, she said, "Mama, the duke is most certainly a gentleman, and would do nothing to force me against my will." He had not, after all; when she had refused him, he had left her alone without another word.

Lady Sophia hesitated, biting her lip. "Darling, I have often thought you were not . . . not as indifferent to him as you have insisted. Indeed, you seem very aware of him when he is in the room. If your feelings for him are confused, it could cloud your judgment. And his behavior last night . . ."

"He is amusing himself with a light flirtation, nothing more," Antonia said. "As for me, I am quite certain of my feelings for the duke, and quite able to exercise sound judgment. I assure you, Mama, I have no intention of further disgracing my good name by doing anything I ought not." The words should have burned her tongue, she thought wryly—or at least pricked her conscience, considering what she had already done.

The conversation might have continued, but the countess entered the room then. Lady Sophia looked so self-conscious that Antonia was mildly surprised her grandmother did not instantly demand to know what they had been discussing, but it became obvious she had another matter on her mind.

"Antonia, since the weather makes outdoor amusements impossible, I believe you young people will find some enjoyment in arranging the Christmas decorations. A tree was cut some days ago, and Tuffet is having it brought into the drawing room now, along with mistletoe and holly boughs. The maids have spent the past week or so stringing berries and making other decorations, so you need only put them in place."

Antonia would have objected, but before she could the duke entered the room. "An excellent scheme, ma'am. I am glad you have adopted the recent custom of bringing a tree inside; it is especially pleasant in weather such as this."

The matter settled to her satisfaction, Lady Ware nodded. "Since Christmas Eve is day after tomorrow, you should have plenty of time to get the decorations in place."

So Antonia found herself once more thrown into the duke's company. Her grandmother carried her mother off immediately after breakfast, obviously intending to occupy her in another part of the castle, and even the servants made themselves scarce as soon as the couple went into the drawing room to find the tree and promised decorations.

Lyonshall behaved as though nothing had happened the night before. He was very casual, not nearly so intense as he had been during the previous evening.

Antonia could not help but feel grateful for that; she could no longer don her social mask in his company. If he had attempted to make love to her, or even to flirt, she knew she would have betrayed herself. Instead, because he was relaxed and carelessly charming, she was able to be calm herself.

The festive nature of the holiday had its own effect, as well. The sharp scent of holly and of the big spruce tree mingled with the spicy fragrance of potpourri from the bowls the maids had set out in nearly every room, and even as vast as the castle was, the enticing aroma of plum pudding and other dishes being prepared for Christmas dinner drifted up from the kitchen.

The yule log was prepared, candles put into place, and holly boughs arranged to please the eye. The maids had strung berries of different colors for the tree, and Antonia was surprised to find among the other decorations small, exquisitely sewn sachets in various shapes, obviously the work of her grandmother.

"I didn't realize she cared so about the holiday," Antonia murmured as she fingered one lovely, potpourri-filled sachet in the shape of a star. "She must have sewn these sachets every year for a long time. Look how many there are."

"Beautiful work," the duke observed. "It's going to be a fine tree."

Antonia agreed with him. In fact, she had to admit the castle would look and feel quite different once it had donned its holiday dress. Already, the huge drawing room seemed warmer, brighter, the colorful decorations adding light and cheerfulness.

She was beginning to see why her family had loved the castle. There was something stately in the sheer size of the place, and a feeling of permanence in the solid stone walls and floors. This place, she realized, had surrounded the Wingate family for centuries. It had sheltered and protected them, hidden their secrets, housed their happiness, their anger, and their tears.

Ever since the ghostly lovers had appeared the night before, Antonia had been aware of a growing feeling that the castle itself was a living thing. That over the centuries, it had absorbed so much of the Wingate family emotions that it, too, had become part of the family. She almost told Lyonshall of this feeling, but kept it to herself in the end. It sounded very fanciful, she decided.

She and Lyonshall worked together in harmony, and for a time Antonia nearly forgot everything except the pleasure of being in the company of a man who talked to her as an equal. But even as they hung decorations on the tree and argued amiably about their placement, she could not help being wary of his changed attitude. More than once, she caught him watching her, and the brooding look she saw so fleetingly caused tension to steal over her.

To her surprise, he continued to behave casually for the remainder of the day, and she blamed her imagination for the dark expression she had seen. He neither said nor did anything to upset or confuse her. He was pleasant and charming at dinner, even drawing a laugh from Lady Sophia, and when the evening was over he escorted

Antonia to her door and left her there with a composed and polite good night.

Antonia told herself it was all for the best. He had obviously accepted her refusal—or had, at least, realized he was more of a gentleman than he had believed himself to be, and had given up the idea of seduction. But the apparent end of his brief courtship did nothing to ease her chaotic emotions.

Once again, she could not sleep, and though her mind automatically marked the approach of midnight with both anticipation and anxiety, she was nevertheless surprised to turn from the fireplace and see that her ghostly visitor had returned. Her fear of the previous night was absent, but the eeriness of what she saw as she watched him moving about the room had a decided effect on her. She felt almost like an intruder, watching him without his awareness, yet she couldn't force herself to look away.

Just as the night before, he moved around the room restlessly for a time before he eventually headed for the door. She followed without making a conscious decision to do so. In the open doorway of her room, she watched a repetition of the previous night's scene enacted in the hall, and the same sensual awareness stole over her.

The dark man and his fiery-haired lady shared a love that had lived beyond their time, surviving the death of mortal flesh to haunt this hall of stone and silence. No one, Antonia thought, could look upon such unquenchable emotions and not feel the power of them. It made her throat ache, made her peculiarly aware of her own body as her heart beat and the blood coursed through her veins. And it made her feel a profound sense of loss, because she had believed just such a love as theirs had once been within her own grasp. That grief grew even stronger when she saw Lyonshall through the entwined lovers. It was as if fate was mocking her.

She remained unmoving in the doorway as the ghostly pair went into his room. As on the previous night, he closed the door and came to her, but before he could speak she caught a glimmer of movement beyond him in the hallway.

"Look," she murmured.

A third ghostly form had appeared at the end of the hall near the stairs. She came toward them, a pretty woman past the first blush of youth but not yet near middle age, her dress made up of dark colors and fashioned in the style of a century before. She gave a clearer idea of the time than the other two had, since she was fully dressed. She wore a high, stiff cap of frilled linen with a short veil on her neatly arranged dark hair; an outer garment, trailing in back, with semi-long sleeves and linen cuffs, was worn open in front over a laced bodice and flounced skirt.

She was attractive in a colorless way, but seemed far more lifeless than the other two. Like the lovers, she took no notice of the two living spectators. She was moving along the hallway, but stopped when she reached the duke's bedchamber door.

Like a person attracted by some sound, she stood with her head turned a little toward the door and her attention fixed on that room. She was very still for a long moment, the expression on her face curiously intent, even masklike. Then her lips twisted in an ugly grimace, and she continued on her way.

Antonia felt chilled as she watched the woman. It was a feeling quite unlike what she had experienced upon first seeing a ghost in her room. This was something far more acute, and deeply troubling. She had a strange and powerful urge to rush to the lovers and warn them to take care, because someone in the castle intended them harm. She *knew* that somehow, felt it with every fiber of her being. The lovers were in danger.

Her rational mind reminded her that these people had been dead for a hundred years, but she couldn't seem to throw off the oppressive feeling of dread or her anxious desire to prevent a tragedy.

Standing beside Lyonshall, she watched the woman continue down the hallway and vanish into one of the rooms. Slowly, Antonia turned and went into her own room, her emotions so disturbed she didn't realize immediately that Lyonshall had followed her.

"Toni?"

Antonia went to the fireplace, still feeling chilled, and stretched her hands out toward the flames. "That other one," she murmured. "She means them harm."

"Yes, I saw."

"I feel so helpless. It's like watching the first seconds of a carriage accident in the streets and feeling powerless to stop what you know is coming."

He stood several steps away, watching her, and his voice remained low. "Whatever will happen—already *has*, Toni. A hundred years ago."

"So my mind tells me. But what I feel . . . is difficult to overcome. They seemed so happy together, with their whole lives before them, yet I have an awful certainty they didn't live much beyond what we have already seen." Antonia shook her head a little, trying to push away the dread. "I wonder who they were."

"You don't know?"

"No, I—I know very little of my family's history in this place. That is a dreadful thing to say, isn't it?"

"Natural, if you haven't lived here. Most of us do tend to live in the present."

"I suppose."

"Have you asked Lady Ware about the ghosts?" he asked. "She would very likely know the history of the castle, and of the family."

"No," she replied. When he continued to gaze at her with one brow raised, she shrugged. "Grandmother is such a brusque and matter-of-fact person, I have no doubt she would tell me I imagined the whole."

He was silent for a moment, an odd look of hesitation in his eyes. "Somehow I feel sure she wouldn't tell you that. I believe she knows about the ghosts. My valet tells me only the South wing of the castle is held to be haunted. Perhaps Lady Ware put the two of us here for that reason."

"Because of the ghosts?" Antonia frowned. "Why would she do such a thing?"

Again, Lyonshall hesitated. "If she wishes us to reconcile, she may have believed a pair of young lovers might push us in the right direction—even if they are ghostly lovers."

Antonia felt wary, disturbed by the way he had led the conversation back to them. She was in no state to endure more of the previous night's discussion, and she was surprised that he wished to talk about the subject yet again. He had accepted her request to end their engagement with little attempt to persuade her to change her mind, yet now he seemed almost obsessed. She would have thought the blow to his pride—if nothing else—would have made the entire subject unbearable.

She avoided his eyes by turning back to the fire. "I seriously doubt she has any such belief. She told me herself it would be foolish to suppose you would make me a second offer, and she knows very well the idea is—"

"Is what? Repugnant to you?" he demanded when she broke off abruptly.

"Must we discuss this again?"

"Yes. Because you have yet to tell me the truth." His voice was a little harsh now.

Antonia refused to look at him. "I thought you had accepted my wish to have done with this. Your behavior today led me to believe that was so."

He gave a hard laugh. "Indeed? My behavior today, Toni, was due to your refusal last night. No man with any sensibility could accept with pleasure the look of sick anguish I saw on your face last night. If you wished to hurt me yet again, you certainly did."

"That was not my intention," she heard herself say, and wondered why she couldn't allow him to believe even the worst of her if it would only drive him away.

"Then what was your intention? You were willing, Toni, we both know that. You came alive in my arms with all the passion I remember so well, and for a moment I hoped . . . But then you refused me, in a voice so cold it froze my heart. What have I done to earn that from you? How can I accept your wishes when I don't understand the reasons for them? Is my desire to make you my wife so unbearable to you?"

Trying to appear calm even if her mask was gone, Antonia held her voice steady. "If you must hear it again, I have no wish to marry you, Richard. I suppose you feel yourself perfectly entitled to your revenge, but—"

"Revenge?" He crossed the room quickly and grasped her arm, turning her roughly to face him. "Is that why you refused me last night? Because you believe I want revenge? What put such a mad notion as that into your head?"

She met his grim eyes as squarely as she was able, though it required a tremendous effort. "It seems obvious to me. In all the months since our engagement ended, you have made no effort whatsoever to heal the breach, or even expressed interest in doing so—why now? Because you suddenly find yourself virtually alone with me and stormbound? No, I think not. You wish to punish me for jilting you. I realized that last night. Why else would you go to such lengths to remind me that I gave up to you what any woman should give only on her wedding night? Why else would you torment me with the knowledge of how—how easily I can be swayed when you touch me?"

A crooked smile curved his lips briefly. "At least you admit that much. So I wasn't wrong, after all. You do still want me, don't you?"

"Should I deny it?" she said bitterly. "What good would that do? You know the truth."

"I know another truth, Toni." His voice was as implacable as it had been the night before. "You could not feel desire—if you didn't feel love as well. You don't hate me. You might wish to hate me, but you can't."

It was like being kicked in the stomach, and for a moment Antonia could not breathe. The last of her defenses collapsed into painful rubble. She felt horribly powerless, and her heart ached with its every beat. To love a man she could not trust was bad enough; to know that he was certain of her love was even worse. It was what she had struggled to hide from him— all for naught. Lying now was something she hadn't the strength or will to do.

Finally, in little more than a whisper, she said, "Then it appears your revenge is complete, doesn't it?"

His free hand lifted to touch her face, and his voice softened to a deep, husky note. "I don't want revenge, I want you to be my wife. We belong together, Toni, don't you see? Can't you feel that as surely as I do? Give me your love as well as your passion. We can put the past behind us and start again."

She realized then that the stormy gray of his eyes was a sign of determination rather than anger; he really *did* want to marry her. But that knowledge did little to ease her pain. She loved him, and she wanted him, but she did not trust him not to hurt her again.

She dared not trust him.

"Thank you for the honor," she said politely, "but I must refuse."

The softened expression left his face, replaced by a hard mask of resolve. His big hands gripped her shoulders, the fingers almost painful as they held her. "Why? This time I mean to get the answer, Toni, and I won't give up until I do. Why won't you marry me?"

She was too tired to avoid the answer, even to

spare herself the pain of his lies. "Perhaps it really did mean nothing to you; that is always the defense I hear of gentlemen. But it meant something to me. And even more than that betrayal, you destroyed my trust in you with your lies. How could I marry a man I no longer trusted?"

A swift frown drew his brows together, and she could have sworn his voice was sincerely bewildered when he said, "Lies? What are you talking about?"

"Mrs. Dalton," she replied flatly.

Three

"Claire Dalton?" His frown deepened. "What do you know of her?"

"More than you intended for me to know, I should say." Antonia smiled thinly. "She was—and perhaps still is—your mistress."

Richard released her shoulders and stepped back. His eyes narrowed, and he spoke very deliberately. "She was. However, since my—arrangement with her ended before I asked you to be my wife, I hardly see why it would concern you."

"If it *had* ended, you are quite right. But it didn't end."

"Toni, I am telling you it did."

Antonia had known it would hurt to hear him lie, and she had not been wrong. It hurt dreadfully. She half-turned away from him, her back to the fire, and she could feel her face harden with aversion. "Of course it did," she said tonelessly. "After all, no lady must ever acknowledge the existence of such a creature. She turns her head away, or makes herself blind to that—unbearable reality."

"Toni—"

"Please, no more lies."

"I am not lying to you."

"No?" She looked at him. "Can you tell me you haven't seen her since our engagement was announced?"

He hesitated, then cursed roughly under his breath. "No, I can't tell you that. If you must have the truth, our relationship resumed briefly—*after* you ended the engagement. But I swear to you, I didn't see her while you were promised to me, nor would I have gone to her after our marriage. I wanted no mistress, Toni, only you."

"I don't believe you." Her lips curved in a painful little smile. "You see? You swear to me,

76

and I can't believe it. You tell me you speak the truth, and I hear lies. I don't trust you, Richard. Imagine the hell you would live in with a wife who called you a liar."

He shook his head slowly, a muscle leaping in his tight jaw. "Why can't you believe me? Who told you about Claire?"

"She did."

"What?" He took a step and grasped her shoulders again, turning her fully to face him. "How came you even to speak to her?"

"Worried about my ladylike sensibilities?" She laughed without amusement. "I must admit, my mother would have considered my visitor—quite shocking. But Mrs. Dalton found me alone when she came to see me that morning. I was waiting for you, already in the parlor. A housemaid answered the door, and I am afraid she had no idea that the very fashionable lady who wished to see me was nothing of the kind."

His hands tightened on her shoulders. "What did she say to you?"

"What do you think? She congratulated me on our forthcoming marriage. I needn't concern myself with her, she said. She would take up very little of your time. Just as she had during the past months."

"And you believed her? Toni, how could you take the word of a spiteful woman over mine?"

Antonia jerked away from him. She went to her dressing table and opened the jewelry case atop it. Finding what she sought, she returned to Richard and held out her hand. The firelight reflected off the object she held, glinting brightly gold.

"Because *she* had proof," Antonia said raggedly.

He lifted the object from her trembling hand. It was a watch fob, made quite simply; its only decoration was a golden button engraved with the letters AW.

"You have reminded me so often of that day in the stable," she said, her voice still unsteady. "Do you remember? Do you remember how . . . in our haste . . . a button was torn off my riding habit? We laughed about it later. You said you would keep it, as a treasured memento of our first time together. You had this fob made, and you wore it often. Your *mistress* was kind enough to return it to me."

"She had this?" His face was curiously pale.

78

"She told you I had given it to her? Toni, she lied, I swear to you. She must have . . . My house was robbed while we were at the theater together the night before; she must have hired the thief—"

"Please, don't! I have heard enough lies."

His hand closed hard over the fob, and his eyes darkened almost to black. "I am telling you the truth. If you had not left London so quickly, you would surely have heard of the robbery—the news was all over town."

"And was it all over town that we were lovers?" Tears burned her eyes, and she struggled not to shed them. "She told me that, as well. How the two of you laughed at my—my innocence. How you compared me to her . . . and found me sadly lacking."

"No." He lifted his hand jerkily toward her face. "My God, Toni, I would never have done such a thing! You have to believe me."

She backed away, her movements as jerky as his. "I wish I could. I—I really do. But I can't. Please, just leave me alone."

His hand fell to his side, and he stared at her for a long time in silence. "You won't believe me no matter what I say, will you? She poisoned you completely against me."

Antonia's eyes flicked to the watch fob he still held in his hand, then returned to his face. "Good night, Richard."

He must have realized she was a whisper away from breaking down, or perhaps, as he had said, knew that she was simply unable to listen to any more, at least for the moment. Still holding the fob, he went to the open door. He hesitated there briefly, looking back at her with a grim expression, then went out of the room and closed the door quietly behind him.

Antonia's control lasted no longer than that. She found her way to the bed, though it was impossible to see through the flood of tears, and sat down before her legs could no longer support her. She felt that she had turned her back on something infinitely precious, and the grief and pain tore at her as if they were living creatures with talons.

But she couldn't have acted in any other way; she knew that. Without trust, there was no possibility of happiness; eventually, her love would be destroyed by mistrust, and a marriage with Richard would end up worse even than the hollow relationships that passed so often for marriages.

She had no idea how long she sat there, but gradually the tears slowed to a trickle and then ceased. The fire was dying, the room growing chilly—or perhaps that was only a miserable coldness caused by the emptiness inside her. Either way, she realized vaguely that she should go to bed, and tried to summon the energy to do so.

She raised her bowed head, and then went very still as she stared across the room. She was so numb that all she felt was faint surprise and a remote curiosity.

This young woman ghost was neither the fiery-haired enchantress nor the malevolent darker woman. She somewhat resembled the man, with her brunette hair and thin, sensitive face, but her style of clothing seemed to indicate she had lived at least a score of years after him: her gown was simpler in design, with a fuller shorter skirt, which did not trail along behind her, and she wore no cap. She stood in the center of the room, and her gentle, tragic eyes were fixed on Antonia.

"You know I am here," Antonia said slowly, a tiny chill of fright feathering up her spine. "You are . . . aware of me."

The woman smiled and nodded, then stepped back and made a beckoning gesture.

Antonia wanted to refuse, but found herself unable to do so; again, she seemed to be in the grip of a compulsion. She rose and followed as the woman led her out of the room and a little way down the hall. Turning to look at her, the woman gestured again, toward Lyonshall's door. It was a simple gesture, an invitation to enter.

The urge to obey—combined with Antonia's own longings—was so strong she actually took a step in that direction. But then she stopped and shook her head. "I can't," she said in a voice hardly louder than a whisper. "I can't go to him."

The woman gestured again insistently, clearly much distressed, her sorrowful eyes almost pleading.

Though she had thought herself emptied of tears, Antonia felt them stinging her eyes again. "No, I can't. It hurt so much when he lied to me—I am afraid to trust him again."

After a moment of obvious indecision, the woman's hand fell to her side. She moved away from the duke's door and beckoned again.

With a feeling of unreality, Antonia followed.

She didn't know where she was being led; though she had explored the castle a few times during her childhood, that had been many years ago when the South wing had been shut up, and she had made no attempt to explore the wing on this visit. The wide corridors were utterly silent, the stone floor chilly beneath her slippered feet, but she kept her gaze fixed on the slightly hazy form of her guide.

Sconces lined only the main corridor where Antonia and the duke were quartered; the numerous other hallways and galleries, unoccupied, were dark. When her guide left the main corridor behind, Antonia had the eerie feeling of being swallowed up by darkness and silence.

"Wait! I can't see you!" She took several hurried steps, more by instinct than sight, then slowed in relief as she saw her guide waiting for her.

The woman had paused at the head of a short hallway leading to a window, and gestured toward a table against the wall. Gratefully, Antonia lit the oil lamp there, then walked a bit quicker to keep her guide safely within the circle of yellow light as they continued down the hallway. The woman stopped about halfway, and turned to indicate a large portrait hanging between two doors.

Antonia stepped closer, holding the lamp high, and gasped aloud. One of the lovers was beautifully represented, her fiery hair brilliant and her delicate face glowing with life. Formally dressed with her hair piled high atop her small head, she looked almost regal. Her gown was green velvet, the color bringing out faint flecks of green in her big eyes. There was a quantity of lace at her wrists and throat, a heart-shaped patch at one corner of her smiling lips, and an enormous emerald ring glowed on the index finger of her right hand.

Antonia could see the resemblance to herself more clearly in the painting, and for a moment she had the eerie thought that she was the reincarnation of this fragile, doomed creature.

There was a brass nameplate on the frame, and she read it aloud. "Linette Dubois Wingate." She looked up at the face again, then turned to find her guide pointing at another painting directly across the hall. When Antonia moved a few steps in that direction, the lamplight revealed a portrait of the man.

Like Linette, he was dressed formally though

his dark hair was unpowdered. His coat was a heavy brocade shot through with gold thread, and both his cuffs and cravat were lace-edged. There was strength in his thin face, honesty in the level gaze of his eyes, and the sensuality Antonia knew him capable of was evident in the curve of his lips. According to the name-plate, his name had been Parker Wingate.

After a moment, she followed her beckoning guide a little further down the hall, and found herself gazing at a portrait of the guide herself. It had obviously been painted when she was a girl on the brink of womanhood, yet the eyes in that gentle face were already shadowed with sorrow.

"Mercy Wingate," Antonia read aloud. She studied the portrait for several minutes, then turned to look at Mercy's hazy form just a few steps away. "You were—their daughter?"

Mercy nodded. She beckoned again, turning back the way they had come, and Antonia followed obediently. When they reached the head of the corridor, she kept the lamp, partly because Mercy went on without pausing. It appeared she was bound for the central part of the castle. Antonia was led to the library on the ground floor, and to a certain area of the shelves.

Her guide pointed to a particular book, then retreated as Antonia went to the shelf and set her lamp on a nearby table. She had to reach above her head, but managed to get the book.

It was a thick volume bound in fine leather and stamped with gold. A book that had been privately printed in the very year of Antonia's birth. She touched the title stamped simply into the cover. *"Wingate Family History.* But—" She turned to speak to her guide, and found herself alone in the huge, silent room.

For a few moments, Antonia stood there questioning herself. It had been real, not a dream, she was sure of it. She *felt* it. She had not walked in her sleep; she had been unaware of the book's existence, so why—and how—would she have dreamed of it? Nor had she known of the portraits, since she had never seen them before; they must have been in storage in the South wing, or else had hung on the walls all the time the wing had been closed off.

No, Mercy had been as real as the ghostly representations of her parents that Antonia— and Richard—had seen during the past two nights. Eerie and strangely compelling in her sorrow and gentleness, she had stepped out of the past because . . . Why? Different from the others, she had been fully aware of Antonia, even communicating with her, however silently. She had been obviously distressed by Antonia's refusal to go into Richard's room, and Antonia had to believe that Mercy had been in some way trying to help them.

Antonia had many questions; she only hoped that the book would provide at least a few answers. She picked up the lamp and, carrying the heavy volume, made her way slowly back to the South wing and her bedchamber.

Weary though she was, the disturbing events and her chaotic emotions made sleep impossible, so she took the book with her to bed and began reading. The writer who had been commissioned to write the history knew his job well; with dry facts gleaned from family records, letters, and journals, he wove together a straightforward narrative that proved to be interesting, often entertaining, and sometimes tragic as he explored centuries of one family's existence.

There was even a family tree, and Antonia studied it for a long time before she went further. She found two shocks there. The date of a death was one. The other was her own lineage: she was a direct descendent of the sad guide— and the lovers. With a better understanding now of her resemblance to Linette, Antonia turned past the family tree and began reading.

Finding herself caught up in the story of the earliest Wingates, she found it difficult to force herself to skip ahead to the previous century, but her curiosity and unease about the young couple was too powerful to deny. She located the correct section dealing with the parents of Parker Wingate, and began reading there.

Theirs was an interesting time, full of historical events as well as the usual details of family life. Antonia enjoyed reading about all of it. As it had been the night before, she remained awake until nearly dawn, finally giving in to sleep still half-sitting up against the pillows with the heavy book across her knees.

Physical and emotional exhaustion had taken their toll; she slept deeply.

Antonia slept through the morning and well into afternoon, waking finally to see her maid sitting peacefully before the fire with a pile of mending in her lap.

"Good heavens," Antonia murmured, sitting up. "What time is it? I feel as if I have slept for days."

"No, milady, only for hours. It is after three."

While Antonia was coping with that slight shock, Plimpton went to the door, opening it just a crack and speaking to someone outside. The conversation was brief, and Plimpton soon returned to the bed. "One of the girls was so obliging as to wait until you should awaken, milady, since I did not wish to leave you. She will bring up your coffee, and you shall have it in bed."

"I have been in bed long enough," Antonia protested.

"Milady, you were worn down yesterday, and spent the better part of the night, I believe, reading that huge book. Her ladyship has been here, and she agrees with me that you should not get up before dinner."

"But—"

"She insists, milady. As do I." Briskly, Plimpton helped Antonia to bank her pillows and offered a damp cloth to wash her face and hands. By the time the coffee arrived, Antonia was more wide awake, and looked presentable enough to receive visitors, should any arrive.

Plimpton, always good company, served her mistress coffee and then returned to her mending, willing to remain silent unless Antonia desired conversation.

It was rare for Antonia to keep to her bed for any reason, but she was glad enough to obey on that afternoon. With no need to keep up her composure for the benefit of probing eyes, she felt much less strained, and she was glad of the opportunity to continue reading the family history—both out of real interest and a desire to keep her thoughts away from Richard.

That wish, however, proved futile. Antonia had fallen asleep last night in the middle of the account of Parker Wingate's early years, and she soon reached the section dealing with his engagement to a young French girl; Linette Dubois was, in fact, his distant cousin, and had come to stay at the castle the previous spring.

The author of the history had obviously found the young lovers' story touching; it seemed he had discovered journals written by both of them that provided him with a wealth of details. No other section of the book was so painstakingly recounted as the brief, tragic love story.

Antonia could not help thinking of Richard as she read. She could not help aching as the lovers' own words about one another recounted a depth of emotion that was so powerful and intimate it had transcended time itself. They had intended to wed just after the new year, but their passion had been too intense to deny; they had become lovers—as noted in both their journals—the week before Christmas.

As Antonia and Richard had witnessed, Linette and Parker had met each midnight hour after the remaining family members were asleep in their rooms, spending the bulk of the night in her room because, as Parker had dryly noted in his journal, it was a much simpler matter for a man to don his dressing gown and slip back across the hall in the silent hours before dawn than for a lady to do so.

Antonia had to smile at that, but then she turned the page and discovered an abrupt, chilling, and inexplicable end to the lovers' happiness. As she read the few remaining paragraphs, she shared the author's sense of grief and tragic waste, as well as his obvious bafflement.

Only the events were known; the actions

and results were without the motivations and causes.

"Milady? Do you feel faint?"

She looked up to find Plimpton hovering anxiously, and supposed that she must have gone pale. "I know what happened, and when," she murmured, "but I don't know *why*."

"Milady?"

Antonia shook her head. "Nothing. I am quite all right, really. What time is it? I should dress for dinner."

"We can have a tray brought up, milady—"

"No. No, I had better go down, or Mama will be convinced I am ill."

"Very well, milady," said Plimpton, clearly unconvinced. "I will draw your bath."

Just over an hour later, Antonia encountered Richard waiting at his door to escort her, and felt a pang when she saw that he was wearing the button fob. His eyes were unreadable when they met hers.

"Good evening, Toni," he said quietly, offering his arm.

For an instant, she hesitated, but she seemed to have no more power over her longing to be near him than she had had over the compulsion to follow a ghost through the darkened corridors of the castle.

"I trust you are feeling better," he said as they walked down the hallway together.

"I was not ill, merely tired." Quite suddenly, Antonia had a vision of years to come, of meeting him socially and behaving with this horrible stilted politeness, and her very heart seemed to wrench in pain.

How could it all have gone so wrong?

He might have been thinking similar thoughts. His voice was very even when he said, "As soon as the weather clears sufficiently, I will remove myself. I am sure you don't believe this, but I have no wish to distress you any further."

Not trusting herself to speak, Antonia merely nodded. She walked beside him, her head a little bowed, and wondered vaguely if the Wingates had always been unlucky in love. It seemed so. It seemed so indeed.

She was never able to recall afterwards how she managed to get through the evening. She remembered nothing of conversations, though knew she must have spoken because neither her grandmother nor her mother seemed to find anything amiss. She recalled only the long, slow walk with Richard back to her room late in the evening, and the stiffly polite good nights at her door.

She changed into her nightclothes and firmly sent Plimpton off to bed. Expecting another ghostly encounter, she didn't go to bed herself, but sat by the fire reading the account of Mercy Wingate's childhood, marriage—and tragically young death. It was not the best of stories to read while alone, and she was actually a bit relieved when a soft knock fell on her door a little before midnight.

It was Richard, of course, and his voice held the same quiet note as before, "I doubt either of us is in any mood to observe yet another passionate embrace in the hallway, however ghostly."

Without even thinking of suggesting that he wait somewhere else, Antonia nodded and stepped back, leaving the door open as he entered. She returned to her chair by the fire, torn between her longing to be with him and the pain it caused. What she should have done, she knew, was to have moved to another room long since, but that had only just occurred to her.

"I believe they will both be in this bedroom tonight—at least for a time," she said. "If, that is, they are reenacting the events of their lives."

"How do you know that?" Richard asked as he came to stand near the fireplace.

Antonia touched the book on a small table by her chair. "I have been reading about them in this book of family history. Their account was based largely on their own journals." She frowned briefly. "I must ask Grandmother if the journals still exist; I would like to read them."

"So would I." He hesitated, then added, "Though, of course, I will be gone soon."

Antonia experienced another sudden flash of memory. It was early in their engagement, when he had taken her to visit the British Museum, and they had scandalized several other visitors by holding hands and ruthlessly criticizing the various works of art. Since both were playfully engaged in trying to outdo each other, their remarks had become so outrageous that one middle-aged lady had sat down plump upon a bench and declared that she had never been more shocked in her life.

Recalling their laughter now, Antonia felt a throb of bittersweet pain. "Richard—" she began impulsively, then broke off when she caught a glimpse of movement near the bed.

It was Parker Wingate, restlessly awaiting the hour of his rendezvous with Linette. They watched as he moved about the room. Richard nodded when Antonia identified him by name.

"Who is the lady?" he murmured.

"Linette Dubois, a distant cousin. And his betrothed."

Antonia had no sooner spoken than Linette entered the room. Parker turned, obviously surprised, and she lifted a finger to her lips in a conspiratorial manner, her delicate face alight with mischief and love.

"I suppose," Richard remarked, "they both consider it less improper for a man to visit a lady's bedchamber than vice versa."

He had read their expressions accurately, Antonia thought, and nodded in agreement. Then she forgot everything except the sweet tenderness of the scene they were witnessing.

Linette went to her betrothed and lifted one of his hands in both of hers. She rubbed his hand briefly against her cheek and kissed it, while he stood gazing down at her bowed head with an expression so filled with love and desire, Antonia's throat tightened. He said something to her, and she looked up with a gentle smile before reaching into the pocket of her dressing gown.

A moment later, she placed a gold, heart-shaped locket into his hand. She opened it and showed him the curl of her fiery hair lying inside, then closed it again and stood on tiptoe to put the chain around his neck. She kissed him very tenderly. He held her close for a long moment, then lifted her into his arms and carried her from the room.

"Toni, love, don't," Richard said huskily, and only then did Antonia realize she was crying.

"You don't understand." Huddled in her chair, she felt overpowering grief, for them and for all lovers torn apart. "Tomorrow is Christmas Eve. That is when it happens, tomorrow night." She covered her face with her hands, unable to hold back a jerky sob. "Oh, God, how could it go so wrong for them? How could it go so wrong . . . for us?"

He made a rough sound and came to her, grasping her arms and drawing her up from the chair. "Please don't, sweetheart, I can't bear it. I have never seen you cry before." His voice was still husky, and the arms that held her close were gentle yet curiously fierce.

Antonia couldn't stop; she sobbed against his broad chest in a storm of grief. Gradually, however, she became aware of his murmurs, the hard warmth of his body, and the strength of his arms around her. She was still aching, but instinct warned her that she had to withdraw from him before her churning emotions sparked another kind of storm.

Finally, she was able to raise her head, but before she could speak he surrounded her face with his hands, thumbs gently brushing away the last of her tears.

"Toni . . ."

He was too close. His face filled her vision, her heart, her soul. The tenderness in his eyes was her undoing. She tried, but there was no force, no certainty, behind her murmured plea.

"Please . . . please just go."

At first, it seemed he would. But then his face tightened, and his head bent toward hers. "I can't," he whispered just before his lips touched hers. "I can't walk away from you again."

Antonia couldn't ask him a second time. The first touch of his mouth brought all her senses alive, and though some tiny part of her consciousness whispered of regrets, she stopped listening. The sadness of the tragedy awaiting the ghostly lovers had made her own painful love more acute than ever before. She would take what she could, if only for a night.

He kissed her as if he felt the same desperate need, his mouth slanting over hers to deepen the contact and his arms drawing her even closer to his hard body. She felt the thick silk of his hair under her fingers, and realized only then that she had slid her arms up around his neck. A fever of desire rose from the core of her, spreading outward until all she knew was heat and yearning.

She was kissing him back and, just as in that snug stable so many months ago, she forgot she was a lady and knew only that she was a woman.

She murmured a wordless protest when his lips left hers, but shivered with pleasure at their velvety touch on her neck. His hands untied the ribbons of her dressing gown, and she shrugged the garment off blindly.

"Toni . . . let me love you, sweetheart . . ."

She didn't answer him aloud, but when his

lips returned to hers he didn't have to ask again. His tongue slipped into her eager mouth and stroked hers, and his hands moved down her back to cup her bottom, the fine cambric of her nightgown providing a soft friction between her flesh and his. Antonia could feel her entire body molding itself to his as if it were boneless, and the hardness of his arousal made her achingly aware of the emptiness inside her. Her breasts were pressed to his chest and they were throbbing, swelling with the need for his touch.

She wanted him to touch her, wanted to feel his hands on her naked flesh. It was an overpowering desire, a necessity so intense that nothing else mattered to her except the satisfying of it. She felt him lift her, carry her a few steps, and then the softness of the bed was beneath her.

Her eyes still closed and her mouth fierce under his, she pulled impatiently at his dressing gown until he wrestled the garment off. For a while then, she didn't know who was doing what, only that her nightgown vanished and she felt the sensual shock of his flesh against hers.

In the stable, they had not completely undressed; the shortness of their time together and their haste to have one another had made that a luxury they could ill afford. But now they had the night and assured privacy, and Antonia wanted to cry or laugh aloud at the glorious freedom.

A little moan escaped her when he trailed his lips down her throat, and she forced her eyes to open. He was looking down at her naked body, his eyes dark and on his hard face an expression of wonder she had seen only once before.

"Toni . . . Oh, God, you're so beautiful . . ."

Antonia felt no embarrassment, and not even a hint of shame, no matter what the whispery voice of her ladylike upbringing insisted. She was glad he found her beautiful, glad that her body pleased him. Her hands touched his broad shoulders, the strong column of his neck, and then her fingers slid into his hair as his head bent to her again.

His lips trailed over the satiny slope of her breast, and then she felt the burning pleasure of his mouth closing over her tight nipple. She cried out in surprise, her body arching of its own volition, stunned by the waves of sensation washing over her. His hand was stroking and kneading her flesh, his mouth hungry on her nipple, and she knew he could feel, perhaps even hear, the thundering beat of her heart.

Heat built in her, burning, and she couldn't seem to hold her body still. His hand slid slowly down her belly, making all her muscles quiver, and when he touched the burnished red curls over her mound her entire body jerked at the shock of pleasure. Her legs parted for him, and his hand cupped her, one finger probing gently.

Antonia moaned wildly, all her consciousness focused on his hand and mouth, and the surging response of her body to his skilled touch. He was caressing her insistently, stroking her damp, swollen flesh until she didn't think she could bear another moment of the coiling tension. It was pain, yet it was pleasure, and she shuddered at the vast, engulfing sensations.

"Richard . . . please . . . I can't . . ."

She heard her own thin voice as if from a great distance. Mutely, she tugged at his shoulder, and almost sobbed when he immediately shifted his weight to cover her tense, trembling body. She felt the hard, blunt prodding of his manhood, and then the shockingly intimate sensation of her passage stretching to admit him.

It was . . . not quite . . . painful. She had taken him inside her only once, months before, and he was a big man; it was almost like the first time. She felt smothered for an instant, and tremors shook her as her body accepted him. The stark closeness was shocking, but her intense satisfaction when he settled fully into the cradle of her thighs pushed everything else aside. She could feel him, deep inside her, and his heavy weight on her was a pleasure beyond words.

His arms went underneath her shoulders to gather her even closer, and a shudder shook his powerful frame. "You feel so good, sweetheart," he whispered, and his jaw tightened when she moved slightly beneath him. "God, Toni—" His mouth took hers hungrily, and he began moving.

Antonia was lost, and didn't care. She held him, moved with him, her body matching his rhythm with female instincts as old as the caves. The tension wound tighter and tighter, gripping all her muscles while the rising fire burned her senses. It was like being in some desperate race she had to win no matter what the cost to her pounding heart and striving body.

She heard her voice moaning his name, and she thought she kept telling him she loved him over and over, but she was kissing him so wildly that she wasn't sure the words were anywhere except in her feverish mind. There was an instant of something like terror when she lost all control in the helpless wash of feelings. Then even that was submerged beneath waves and waves of pulsing ecstasy. She whimpered into his mouth, her eyes opening as her body carried her far, far beyond herself, and pleasure exploded everywhere.

Crying, she kissed him wildly and held him with the last of her trembling strength as he groaned and shuddered with the force of his own release.

In the stable, the aftermath of their loving had been cut short because of the groom's expected return, but there was no need for haste now. Antonia lay close beside him, in his arms, the covers drawn up over their cooling bodies. The fire was dying in the hearth, but the lamps were still lit, and a soft glow filled the room.

She looked at her hand resting possessively, trustingly, over his hard chest, saw her fingers move caressingly in the thick mat of springy black hair—and she had never felt so confused in her life. What had she done? Swept away by desire for the second time in her life . . .

"Toni?"

"Hmmm?"

"I love you."

She tilted her head back and found him gazing at her steadily, his eyes so tender it made her heart ache. There was only one response she could give him, because there was nothing left except the truth. "I love you, too," she said simply.

He touched her cheek, then shifted slightly, raising himself on one elbow so that he could see her face more clearly. "Don't say it like that, sweet—as if it hurts you to love me."

The conflict within her was plain in her voice. "It did hurt me once. It hurt me so much I can still feel the pain. That hasn't changed, Richard. I'm afraid to trust you."

There was something a little bleak in his eyes now. "All I can do is give you my word that she lied, Toni."

"I know." She didn't have to say it aloud, that his word wasn't enough. They both knew. She had to feel trust, and nothing he could say would repair what had been shattered.

He was silent, gazing down at her, stroking her cheek. "When you told me that morning it was over, all I could think, all I could feel was the shock and pain. You were suddenly a stranger, so filled with hate and bitterness that every word you spoke was like a knife. I didn't know what went wrong, but I could see you were unwilling to talk about it. So I did as you demanded."

His mouth twisted. "I didn't expect you to leave London immediately, nor stay away so long. And when you refused to see me, when my letters were returned unopened . . . What was I to do, Toni? Make a fool of myself by chasing after you like a lovesick boy?"

"No, of course not," she murmured, admitting that he had been put into an impossible situation. With the gawking eyes of society fixed on him, he could hardly have done anything except what he had done—behave like a gentleman.

He bent his head and kissed her, very slowly

and thoroughly, until she felt more than a little dizzy. When he drew back at last to look at her, she had to fight the urge to pull him down to her again. The first tingles of feverish need were stirring in her body once more, and it was difficult to think of anything else.

"You avoided me for so long," he said huskily. "Then my father died less than two months later, and I barely had time to think for nearly a year. Settling the estate seemed to require all my time and energy. At least it kept me too busy to feel very much. But I couldn't forget you, sweet. The scandal had died down, and I hoped there was still a chance for us. I dared not try to see you alone, but I knew we would attend many of the same parties.

"So we did, at the beginning of this season. You at least spoke to me—however stilted and formal those conversations were. And I knew, by then, that you had refused several offers after our engagement ended. But you treated me like a stranger. We were never alone long enough for me to even begin to ask you what had gone wrong."

"Is that why you accepted Grandmother's invitation to come here?" she asked.

He hesitated, clearly trying to decide something. He choose his words carefully. "I came here because it seemed the last chance to heal the breach between us. And because Lady Ware was certain you still loved me."

Four

It was not, perhaps, as great a shock as it might have been. Antonia had long since begun to wonder about her grandmother's motives.

"She told you that?"

Richard nodded. "Her letter was—rather extraordinary. Very blunt and quite assured. She said that she was utterly convinced you were still in love with me, and that if I wished to repair—her term—our relationship, the holidays would present the best opportunity in which to do so."

Almost to herself, Antonia murmured, "How

did she know? She left London shortly after I did, and I saw her only a few times afterward. She seemed disgusted by my—my want of conduct, but never inquired into my feelings."

"Perhaps she didn't need to. You may have given yourself away, love, without knowing. Lady Ware is very wise, I think, and unusually observant."

"So she took matters into her own hands." Antonia was not comfortable with the idea of another's hand steering her fate, and her feelings were plain in her voice.

He smiled. "I am afraid I can feel only gratitude to her. She gave me the opportunity I wanted so badly. Toni . . . take a chance on me, please. Let me prove to you that you can trust me. Marry me."

Antonia stared up at him, biting her bottom lip. She was still afraid to marry him, shying away from her own mistrust, and with that realization came the true enormity of what she had done. "Oh, God," she whispered.

Obviously trying for lightness, he said, "I don't believe a proposal calls for divine assistance."

She laughed, but it was a sound of controlled

desperation. "How could I have allowed this to happen? I have behaved like a jade, a—a whore."

Richard's smile disappeared. "By giving yourself to a man you love?"

"By giving myself to a man I won't marry! A man who lied to me, hurt me . . ."

His lean face tightened. "We always return to that, it seems. What can I do to atone for this betrayal you believe me guilty of? Do you want to hear me beg, is that it?"

"No, I don't want to hear you beg." She would have turned her face away, but his hand held her still. "But I can't pretend a trust I don't feel. Nor can I believe the result would be anything but unhappiness if I married you without trust."

He hesitated, then said ruthlessly, "This is the second time you have lain with me, Toni. What if I have gotten you with child? Will you still refuse to marry me then?"

She closed her eyes. The possibility had already occurred to her. She couldn't help remembering the week after their engagement had ended—the longest week of her life—when she had waited anxiously to discover if their lovemaking had resulted in a child. It had not happened then, but there was every possibility it had happened now.

"Toni, look at me."

Entirely against her will, she met his gray eyes. "I don't know," she whispered. But she did know. If she became pregnant, she would have no choice but to marry him. She would never bring such shame to her family as to bear an illegitimate child—and he would never allow his child to be born without his name.

"*I* do know." His eyes were glittering strangely, and his voice was grim. "I don't want to force you, and if I believed you would be truly unhappy with me, I wouldn't force you no matter what. But I don't believe that, Toni. We love each other, and that love *may* have created a child. If nothing else will persuade you, then that possibility should. You will marry me. If I have to remain in this bed with you until every soul in the castle knows it, then I will."

In an instinctive movement, she tried to pull away from him, but he held her firmly. "No! Richard, you wouldn't—"

"Wouldn't I? There is nothing I can say to make you trust me; very well, then—I will forego trust for the present. In time, I shall prove you can trust me, if it takes me years to do it. But I won't sacrifice those years. We belong together."

Fighting against his determination was a losing battle, and Antonia knew it. He meant what he said; she could see that in his eyes. He wouldn't hesitate to compromise her, and if he did, her grandmother would escort them to the altar with no loss of time, regardless of Antonia's feelings. She would be the Duchess of Lyonshall before the new year.

"I wish I could hate you," she whispered. "It would be so much easier if I could hate you."

His expression softened, and he bent his head to kiss her. "But you don't hate me, sweet," he murmured against her lips. "And if you would only realize it, you *do* trust me. You could never have lain in my arms a second time without trust."

Before she could examine the suggestion, his mouth began working its magic. Her body heated and began to tremble, and she was kissing him back helplessly. She couldn't seem to think of anything but the building pleasure of his touch. Rational thought vanished beneath overwhelming sensation.

Still kissing her, he found the end of her braid and removed the ribbon, and his fingers combed through her thick hair until it was spread out on the pillow like a shower of fire.

"I have dreamed of you like this," he said huskily, lifting his head to gaze at her burning eyes. "Your beautiful hair unbound, your face soft with yearning, your lovely body trembling with desire. We were always a good match, but never more so than in passion."

Antonia caught what was left of her breath and tried to think straight. "You—you are attempting to seduce me," she accused unsteadily.

For some reason, that amused him. Warm laughter lit his eyes and a crooked smile curved his lips. Gravely, he said, "It would take a ruthless man to seduce a woman against her will. Are you unwilling, sweet?"

She might have forced herself to say yes, but since one of his hands cupped a throbbing breast just then, the only sound she was able to make was a whimper. His long fingers caressed her tingling flesh, stroking and kneading, while his gaze remained fixed on her face.

"I wish you could know how beautiful you are in passion," he murmured, his voice husky again. "How soft your skin feels when I touch it. How the warmth of your body entices me." He lowered his head to tease a tight nipple with his tongue, drawing back before she could do more than gasp, then looked at her again as his hand slid down over her belly.

"Are you unwilling, my darling?" he repeated, just as his probing fingers found her wet heat.

Antonia couldn't answer him. She was staring into his fierce eyes, yet her own were unfocused. Her body had remembered pleasure quickly, and now it was demanding more of it. Of him. She arched upward, offering, pleading. She felt the quickening waves of throbbing pleasure.

He bent his head again and took a nipple into his mouth, wringing a broken cry from her. She was out of control, out of herself, lost somewhere and completely dependent on him to bring her safely back again. It was the most incredible feeling she had ever known, of vast helplessness combined with a strange freedom, as unrestrained as pure madness.

She pulled at his shoulder, moaning, but he resisted, lifting his head again to look at her as his fingers caressed her insistently. She wanted to beg him to stop tormenting her, but then the sensations swept over her with a rush, swamping everything, and she cried out wildly. His mouth captured the sound, taking hers possessively, and a moment later his body covered hers.

Antonia felt him come into her while the spasms of pleasure still rippled through her flesh, and the sensation was so incredibly erotic she cried out again. He took her from one peak of pleasure to another, to the most profound fulfillment she had ever known or imagined was possible.

There was no abrupt dividing line between mindless delight and the return of sanity. When she came back to herself he was still with her, his powerful body heavy on hers with a weight that brought another kind of satisfaction. The muscles of his back and shoulders were damp beneath her hands, and she could feel the faint aftershocks in both their bodies. She could also feel a slight coolness in the room since the covers had been kicked away from them, but she wouldn't have wanted to move even if she had been freezing.

She rubbed her cheek against his without thought, and when he lifted his head she was smiling. It felt strange, that smile, unfamiliar and yet not at all wrong.

He kissed her very tenderly. "God, I love you so much," he said in a low, rough voice. "I will be like your ancestor—even death won't stop me from loving you, wanting you."

There was still a tug of resistance in Antonia's mind, but the pull of him was far greater; she knew that she had surrendered. Being his wife could bring her vast happiness or agonizing pain, but she had no choice except to take the risk. Not because she might have conceived his child, but because the thought of living without him was more unbearable than the possibility of pain could ever be.

She lifted her head from the pillow and kissed him. It was the first time she had ever done that, and she saw the flash of hope in his eyes. It moved her, and made her feel pang of hurt. For him. In that moment she truly believed that he loved her.

"You did seduce me," she murmured, smiling.

His mouth curved in an answering smile. "Were you unwilling, love?"

"No." She brushed a lock of dark hair off his forehead and linked her fingers together behind his neck. "I suppose I must be utterly shameless."

"Never say such a thing about my future wife." He was still smiling, but she felt the tension in his body.

She hesitated. "Richard . . . I can't promise to put the past behind me. I don't know if I can do that. But I will try not to let it ruin the future—"

He stopped her hesitant words with kisses that held more love and tenderness than triumph, and his eyes glowed down at her. "My sweet, I swear you will never regret it."

She almost believed him. "Do you still intend to marry me before the new year?"

"Would you mind that?" His question was serious. "Your grandmother has informed me there is a small church nearby with an obliging vicar."

"Has she, indeed." Antonia's voice was dry.

He smiled slightly. "If you wish, we will announce our engagement for the second time and be wed in London with all the accompanying pomp and ceremony. I own I would prefer a more quiet wedding—and an extended honeymoon. We could travel abroad, perhaps."

Innocently, she said, "Fainthearted, Your Grace?"

His smile turned a bit sheepish. "Well, I admit I would find it less—taxing—to reappear in London next season after the *ton* has had time to become accustomed to our marriage. By then, some other choice morsel of gossip will no doubt command their attention."

Antonia knew how his pride had suffered from the scandal she had caused, and she was grateful to him for not making her feel more guilty about it. He really was a gentleman to the core, she thought—and the first tiny seed of doubt was sown in her mind.

Would a man of such honesty and character have been capable of the magnitude of his betrayal? To not only keep a mistress during their engagement, but also to discuss her and their lovemaking with that woman? To give his mistress a fob he had gone to the trouble of having fashioned from a button torn from his future wife's clothing?

And would *that* man have been so willing, even determined, to offer up his pride in an attempt to woo the lady who had spurned him?

It made no sense, Antonia realized with a jarring shock. The picture painted of him on that bleak day nearly two years before simply did not match what she knew of him—and what she saw of him now.

"Toni, love, if you wish to brave the *ton* in a stupendous London wedding, I am more than willing."

She blinked up at him. "What? Oh—no. No, I would much prefer a quiet wedding. Really."

He frowned slightly. "Then what is wrong? For a moment, you were very far away."

Antonia knew there was an answer, but she had to find it for herself. Only then would she have a chance to rebuild the shattered trust.

She smiled. "I just realized how cool the room has become. One of us should find the blankets. Or . . ."

"Or?" His eyes were darkening.

Antonia moved slightly beneath him, and felt the first feathery pulse of renewing need. "Or," she murmured, and lifted her face for his hungry kiss.

* * *

It was the sense of his absence that woke Antonia hours later, and for some time she lay with a drowsy smile on her lips as morning sunlight slanted through the window. Just like Parker Wingate, Richard had apparently slipped back across the hall to preserve his lady's reputation. Having won her acceptance of his proposal, he was gallant enough not to expose their intimate relationship to the entire castle.

He would have done so, however, Antonia acknowledged wryly, if it had best served his purpose.

Her attention was drawn by the soft sounds of Plimpton entering the room, and a sudden realization caused Antonia to sit bolt upright in bed, the covers clutched to her breasts. Her naked breasts. She looked wildly around, and discovered that both her nightgown and dressing gown lay crumpled on the floor, several feet apart. And far out of reach.

She knew her hair was tumbled about her, the curls unruly from Richard's passionate fingers. Just as the bed was tumbled, one of the blankets having been kicked to the floor and never reclaimed. And both pillows bore clear imprints, which made it blatantly obvious that Antonia had not slept alone.

Antonia's face felt very hot, and she had not the faintest idea what she could possibly say.

Plimpton stood stock-still in the center of the room, her thin form erect and her face expressionless. She looked at the abandoned clothing, then examined the blanket on the floor. Then her thoughtful gaze studied the two pillows. Finally, she looked at Antonia.

To her astonishment, Plimpton's prim lips curved in a smile of immense satisfaction.

"I won five pounds," she said.

Antonia was speechless. She watched as Plimpton gathered up the nightclothes and carried them to the bed. "I beg your pardon?"

Calmly, Plimpton said, "The castle staff placed wagers, milady, on whether you and His Grace would patch things up. Only His Grace's valet and myself were of the opinion that you would. He said by the new year. I said before Christmas."

Antonia eyed her maid severely. "You did, did you? And what made you so certain, pray tell?"

"I knew you loved him."

That statement deprived Antonia of speech for a second time, but she recovered quickly. "It is highly improper for you to be placing bets on my virtue!"

"So it would—if we were speaking of anyone other than your betrothed, milady."

Silenced a third time, Antonia decided somewhat wryly that discretion might well prove the better part of valor. In a haughty tone, she said, "I would be obliged if you would hand me my nightgown."

"Certainly, milady," Plimpton replied. "And I will fetch your hairbrush as well."

Antonia had to laugh. She was still a great deal astonished by Plimpton's approval of her scandalous conduct, but it was certainly a more reassuring reaction than shock and disapproval would have been. And since she had implicit faith in her maid's discretion and loyalty, she was not worried about offensive tales being spread below stairs. In fact, she knew very well that Plimpton would not claim her winnings until Richard and Antonia announced their intention to wed.

While she drank her coffee and prepared to face the day, Antonia considered her doubts of the night before. In the bright light of day, those doubts were even stronger, but she could still reach no resolution in her own mind.

If indeed Mrs. Dalton had set out to deliberately destroy Richard's engagement . . . But it was all so farfetched! *Would* she have gone to such lengths as to hire a thief to break into his house? And how had she known about the fob if he hadn't told her? As far as Antonia knew, only the two of them had known of its significance; anyone else would scarcely have noticed that the fob had been fashioned out of a button.

And how had the woman known Antonia and Richard had been lovers?

She might have guessed, or merely assumed, perhaps. If Mrs. Dalton had found the same pleasure in Richard's arms that Antonia had . . .

Antonia pushed that thought violently aside, feeling a little sick. Just the idea of another woman sharing that with him was almost unbearable.

Antonia's gaze fell upon the book of family history, and she felt a pang of guilt. She had actually forgotten what was to happen tonight, on Christmas Eve. Remembering now, she brooded about it as Plimpton finished dressing her hair, then rose from the table and went to get the oil lamp that still sat on a table near her bed.

"I have to return this," she murmured.

"I can do that, milady."

"No, I will on my way downstairs." She wanted to take another look at the paintings.

She encountered no one, and despite the fact that her previous viewing of the paintings had taken place in almost total darkness, Antonia was able to find the short hallway. The window at the far end let in enough light to see clearly, so she left the lamp on the table.

The portraits looked different in natural light, even more alive somehow. Parker and his Linette seemed to gaze longingly at each other across the hall, their eyes locked. And Mercy seemed less haunted and sad, more at peace, than she had in the dark watches of the night.

Antonia stood gazing at the paintings. For the first time in her life, she was aware of her own connection to the past. The roots of a family went deep, she realized, bonding each person to those who had come before—and to those who would follow.

Perhaps that was why Mercy had appeared

to Antonia, she thought. Family responsibility. Perhaps she had somehow sensed her descendant's unhappiness, and had sought a means of helping her. She might have believed that the story of her own parents' tragedy would help Antonia to avert one of her own.

"But it isn't complete, Mercy," Antonia murmured as she gazed at that gentle face. "I still don't know *why*."

"Toni?"

She half-turned, a bit startled, but smiled as Richard reached her. "Hello."

His slight tension disappeared, and he drew her into his arms for a long kiss. Antonia responded instantly; she had burned her bridges, and there was no resistance left in her.

"Hello," he said, smiling down at her. "What are you doing here all alone?"

"Looking at them."

He kept one arm around Antonia's waist as he turned to study the representations of the two ghosts he had seen.

"What are they doing in this hall if their rooms were ours?" he murmured.

"I don't know. I suppose Mercy might have

moved them here because her room was in this hall."

"Mercy?"

Antonia pointed. "There. She was their daughter. The other night, Mercy led me here, and to the book of family history in the library."

"Why, do you suppose?"

"I was wondering about that just now. She was . . . different, Richard. She saw me, and even managed to communicate without saying anything. She was so sad. I think perhaps she knew I was unhappy, and wanted to help me. She . . . uh . . . wanted me to go into your room."

He lifted an eyebrow at her, his eyes gleaming with amusement. "But you, of course, stubbornly refused."

"Well, yes. So she led me here, and pointed to the paintings. Then she led me downstairs to the library, and showed me the book. After that, she vanished."

Still holding her close to his side, he studied the painting of Mercy again. "She looks like her father more than her mother," he remarked. "So they did marry after all."

Antonia hesitated again. "Actually, they didn't."

He looked at her, then back at the portrait. "Mercy Wingate," he read.

"She married a third cousin who was a Wingate, and who eventually inherited the title. I am a direct descendant." Antonia sighed. "Her maiden name was officially Wingate; Parker's father persuaded the local vicar—somehow—to swear there had been a deathbed marriage between Parker and Linette, so it was officially recorded in the parish records. But a ceremony never took place."

Reaching a logical conclusion, Richard said slowly, "Because Parker died? How?"

Antonia hesitated. "*How* makes no sense, because the *why* is missing. But if they are reenacting what happened then, we may discover the *why* tonight. It happened on Christmas Eve."

He was silent for a moment. "Then we will wait until tonight. Will we see a mystery solved?"

"The author of the history didn't know what happened, and I don't believe the family did either. Linette's journal had no entry for Christmas Eve—or any date after that. According to other family members, she never spoke of what happened. She died when her daughter was only a few months old."

"How did she die?"

"The doctor called it a decline." Antonia kept her voice steady with effort. "Parker's mother was convinced that Linette survived him only long enough to bear their child—and then just made herself die."

"What do you think?"

Antonia looked up at him. "I think so too."

"Love is . . . a very demanding master," Richard said softly.

She rested her cheek against his chest. "Yes," she agreed. "It is."

Various members of the castle staff may have been bowled over by Richard's announcement over breakfast of his and Antonia's forthcoming marriage, and Lady Sophia was certainly so astonished she nearly swooned, but the Countess of Ware merely offered a satisfied smile.

"You planned this to happen," Antonia accused her.

"Only fate arranges the affairs of mortals," her

grandmother replied. "I merely presented the two of you with an opportunity to reconcile and left the matter up to you. I am, however, pleased that you both had the good sense to mend your differences. You obviously belong together."

"Thank you, ma'am," Richard said politely, while Antonia could only stare at her grandmother in surprise.

"Oh, dear," Lady Sophia murmured, her expression still shocked. "I never imagined—that is—Of course, I am delighted for you, darling, if it is truly your wish to marry His Grace." She gave Richard such a doubtful look that he grinned at her.

"I will send word to the vicar," Lady Ware announced. "He has expressed himself perfectly willing to perform the ceremony at whatever day I should care to choose."

Antonia regarded her wryly. "Only fate arranges the affairs of mortals? Am I not to be allowed to set my own wedding day?"

There was a hint of genuine amusement in the countess's normally frosty eyes. "Certainly, Antonia."

Antonia and her betrothed had discussed the subject on their way downstairs, but she saw no need to explain that the duke had gotten his own way. He had stated that he would marry her before the new year, and he would settle for nothing else. So she merely said, "December 31st then."

Lady Sophia was flustered all over again. "Here? Do you mean *this year*? But darling, an announcement! And the banns—"

"I have a special license, ma'am," Richard told her. "We won't need to call the banns."

After an obviously stunned moment, she said sternly, "You were very sure of yourself!"

Richard grinned again. "No, ma'am—merely very hopeful."

Lady Sophia, much ruffled, turned to her amused daughter. "Still, darling—so quickly!"

Glancing at her betrothed, Antonia said dryly, "Mama, I would really prefer *not* to attempt to word an announcement to the effect that the engagement of Lady Antonia Wingate and the Duke of Lyonshall has been resumed."

"Oh, dear! No, I suppose people would think that very odd, indeed. But a spring wedding, darling—"

This time, Antonia very carefully avoided looking at her intended. Considering that they were lovers, a delay even of weeks could prove to be unwise. "We would prefer not to wait so long, Mama. Recall, if you please, that we actually became engaged more than two years ago. Even the most censorious of our acquaintance must surely forgive our impatience now."

"But you haven't even a gown!" Lady Sophia wailed.

"Yes, she has." The countess looked steadily across the table at her granddaughter. "My wedding gown has been perfectly preserved, Antonia, and would fit you quite well, I believe. If you wish . . ."

Antonia smiled. "I do wish, Grandmother. Thank you."

From that point on, Antonia found the day to be a full one. With the wedding set for just days away there were arrangements to be made which required lengthy discussions. Lady Sophia had to be gently soothed by Antonia and charmed by the duke into accepting the hasty wedding. Antonia's efforts met with little success, but when Richard stated that he firmly intended Antonia's mother to live with them at Lyonshall, she was so pleased and moved by his obviously sincere desire that much of her awe of him deserted her.

Since he had found a moment alone with Antonia to make the suggestion to her earlier, she was in perfect accord with this scheme. She and her mother had always gotten along well, and Antonia had no fears about the arrangement.

With the wedding details more or less agreed upon, attention turned to the last remaining preparations for Christmas day. The castle tradition was to celebrate the holiday with a large midday meal and the exchange of gifts—the latter being something of a problem for Antonia. She had gifts for her grandmother and mother, naturally, but she had not expected Richard to be here.

So, while the remaining decorations were put into place and the appetizing scents from the kitchen reminded everyone of the meal to come on the following day, Antonia grappled with her problem. She found it unusually difficult to concentrate, partly because Richard had developed the knack of catching her in doorways underneath the mistletoe, where he took shameless advantage of that particular Christmas tradition.

She discovered early on that his composure was unshakable no matter who happened to observe a kiss or embrace, and that he apparently didn't mind that he so clearly wore his heart on his sleeve. She also discovered that her certainty of Richard's earlier betrayal was growing less and less sure. He was the man she had fallen in love with in the beginning, and she could not reconcile this man with the one who had hurt her so deeply. They might have been two entirely different men—or one man wrongly accused.

She continued to worry over the matter at odd moments, but had reached no certain conclusions by the time they retired to their rooms that night. Obviously mindful of Plimpton's presence in the room, Richard left her at her door with a brief kiss. Antonia nearly told him he needn't have bothered to be so circumspect, but in the end kept her maid's knowledge of their night spent together to herself.

"Did you collect your five pounds?" she asked dryly.

"Yes, milady."

Smiling, Antonia sat at her dressing table while Plimpton brushed her long hair and braided it for the night as usual. Almost idly, she opened her jewelry case and looked over the contents. She had been unable to think of a gift for Richard. He would, no doubt, say that her agreement to marry him was all the gift he wanted—but she knew very well he had a gift for her, because she had seen it under the tree, beautifully wrapped.

Snowbound in a castle in Wales, she could hardly drive to the nearest shop to find something appropriate. Therefore, she had to make do with what was available.

She thought of Linette's locket, a gift from the heart. Antonia had no locket she could give to Richard, but she did have a lovely old ruby stickpin that had belonged to her maternal grandfather, who had worn it in his cravat. Richard often wore a jewel in the same manner when in evening dress, and she knew he favored rubies.

Antonia used a small, carved wooden box in which she usually stored her earrings apart from the rest of her jewelry to hold the stickpin, and a colorful silk scarf with which to wrap the box.

By eleven, Antonia was alone in her room and dressed for bed as usual. Her gift for Richard lay on her dressing table, to be taken downstairs in the morning and placed under the tree. With that problem solved, she found her thoughts wholly occupied with what would happen to the lovers tonight.

It had been in the back of her mind all day, producing a small, cold anxiety. There was nothing she could do, her rational mind insisted. Whatever would happen—already had. Still, she could not help worrying about it.

Outside the castle, the day's cold wind and overcast sky had finally given way to another bleak winter storm, and Antonia shivered as she stood by the fireplace and listened to the wind wail in the night. She was not expecting anything to happen until nearer to midnight, but at a quarter past eleven it began.

She was standing by the fireplace when she caught a glimpse of movement near the door, and when she turned her head a chill went down her spine. It was the dark woman with the curiously fixed expression who had shown herself only once before. She had come into Parker's room.

She stood just inside the door, gazing toward the bed. When Antonia looked in that direction, she felt a faint shock to discover that Parker's bed of a century before was exactly where Antonia's present-day bed was—perhaps it was even the same bed. She couldn't help feeling peculiar at the thought that he might have returned from Linette's room each dawn and crawled into bed with herself.

He was lying there now, wearing his dressing gown as if he had meant to rest for just a few minutes. But he seemed to be asleep. He didn't stir as the dark woman moved slowly to the bed and stood gazing down at him. She was dressed—or partly dressed—in a nightgown so sheer that her body was clearly visible beneath it. She glanced toward the table by the bed, and an odd smile curved her thin lips.

Antonia looked as well, and saw the hazy shape of a mug on the table. She returned her gaze to the woman, puzzled and uneasy. What was the significance of the mug? And why was this woman in Parker's room?

As she watched, the woman bent over the sleeping man and seemed to be searching for something. A moment later, she straightened, a heart-shaped golden locket dangling from her fingers.

"No," Antonia murmured, shocked. "Linette gave that to him. You have no right!"

Like the lovers, the woman showed no awareness of a flesh and blood intruder. She put the chain around her own neck and looked at the locket, then very deliberately opened it and removed the curl of Linette's fiery hair, dropping it to the floor with a scornful expression and then moving as if to grind the token underneath her slipper. She looked back at Parker for a moment, a frown drawing her brows together as he moved his head restlessly.

"Wake up," Antonia murmured, hardly aware she had spoken aloud. She felt a cold, awful foreboding. "Please wake up and stop her."

He continued to move in a sluggish way, his eyes still closed, and Antonia was suddenly sure that the mug had contained something to make him sleep. She was feeling colder by the minute as she watched the woman's nimble fingers untie the string of the sheer nightgown and draw the edges of the material apart to bare full breasts almost to the nipples.

With her dark eyes fixed on the sleeping Parker, the woman moved slowly. She released her hair from its braid and combed it with her fingers, deliberately disarranging it. Her upper body seemed to sway, the gold locket shifting between her pale breasts, and she braced her legs a little apart. Her hands left her hair to slide slowly down her face and throat to her body.

Antonia felt sickened as she watched, feeling the woman's unbalanced hunger so acutely it was as if it were a living thing loose in the room. If the lovers' emotions had been tender and passionate, this woman's need was a dark and twisted thing. And it shocked Antonia on some deep level, so that she had to look away.

She didn't want to look back, but after several long minutes her gaze was pulled entirely against her will. And she felt a little sick, still deeply shocked. The woman was languidly stroking her body now, and even as hazy as she was, it was clear she wore the sleepy-eyed, sated look of a woman who had just experienced the utter pleasure of a physical release. Smiling, still caressing herself, she turned away from the bed.

Antonia glanced at Parker once, seeing him move even more restlessly and open his eyes, but she didn't wait to see if he would get up. Instead, she followed the woman.

It was eleven-thirty.

The woman made a movement as if to open the door, then passed through it. Antonia quickly opened it in reality, but stopped before she could do more than cross the threshold. The woman was directly in front of her, half-turned to face Linette's room across the hall.

Her sheer nightgown gaped open, revealing most of one breast and all of the other, the locket dangling between them. Her hair was tumbled, her heavy-lidded eyes and puffy lips glistening. Her smile was filled with a purely female satisfaction.

To a seventeen-year-old girl who had experienced passion herself, there was no doubt this smiling, sated woman had just come from the arms of a lover. And there was no way Linette could have known that the dark woman had been her own lover. She was standing in the open doorway of Parker's room, from which she had just stepped, and the conclusion was a tragically obvious one.

"No," Antonia whispered. "Oh, no, don't believe it."

But Linette did. Her lovely face was dazed with shock and agony. Her hands lifted in a strange, lost way, and her mouth opened in a silent cry of anguish. Then she stumbled into an unsteady run, heading, not toward the stairs, but toward the other end of the wide corridor.

Antonia spared one glance behind her and saw that Parker was struggling up from the bed. Then she raced after Linette, as unaware of her own cry as she was of the fact that she had passed through the hazy form of the dark woman.

If she had been thinking clearly, Antonia would have realized the uselessness of her action. What she had watched happen had occurred a century before, and no mortal hand could change the outcome. But she was completely caught up in the tragic drama, the players as real to her as they had once been in actuality, and it was sheer instinct that drove her to try to stop what was going to happen.

She thought she heard Richard call out her name as she ran, but her eyes were fixed on Linette's form ahead of her. The distraught young woman might have been running blindly, but Antonia knew she was not. She was running toward the widow's walk.

It was a remnant of the original castle or a fancy of some distant Wingate—Antonia didn't know which. The crumbling stone wall around the small balcony might once have been a parapet designed to protect soldiers standing guard, or it might simply have been a rather plain, low balustrade built to prevent a casual stroller from pitching over and falling to the flagstone courtyard far below. In any case, it had begun to deteriorate more than a century before, and though the wing had been renovated, that exterior balcony had been left to crumble.

A solid wooden door, locked once but now merely barred, gave access to the balcony from the corridor. Linette paused for only a moment, seemingly struggling to open the heavy portal, then passed through. Antonia paused barely as long, desperation lending her the strength to lift the stout wooden bar and open the door.

She had forgotten the storm, and the blast of icy wind was shocking. Snow swirled wildly in the air and crunched beneath her thin slippers as Antonia hurried out—and almost immediately lost her balance.

The balcony was only a few feet in width, though it ran along the castle wall for nearly twenty yards. Snow had piled up against the castle wall in a deep drift, and it was that which caused Antonia to stumble and lose her balance. Two steps out from the door the balcony had been swept clean of snow by the wind—but earlier sleet and freezing rain had coated the rough stone in a sheet of ice—and because its support had been crumbling for a century, the outer edge of the balcony had a slight downward tilt.

Antonia tried to stop herself, but the icy stone gave her no purchase. Her own momentum was carrying her in an inexorable slide toward the low wall.

In a fleeting moment that seemed to stretch into infinity, she saw Linette to one side, collapsed against the wall in a heap of grief and pain. The young woman might have meant to throw herself over the wall; it was impossible to know for sure. She huddled against the rough stones, her frail shoulders jerking as she sobbed.

Then Antonia saw Parker stagger out, his unsteadiness clear evidence of the lingering effects of the drug the dark woman had given him. He called out something, shaking his head dizzily, and lurched toward Linette.

It must have been storming that night too. Parker seemed to slip and slide across the few feet of stone, his arms windmilling. It was clear he was trying to get to Linette, but either his drugged reflexes or the blinding storm made him misjudge the distance and angle. He was moving too fast, sliding wildly toward the wall, and he couldn't save himself.

Linette looked up at the last minute, and what she saw must have haunted her all the remaining months of her life. Her lover hit the wall only a couple of feet from her, and it was too low to save him. He pitched forward, and vanished into the darkness.

Antonia saw all of that in a flashing instant. Then she felt the bite of the wall against her upper thighs, and her momentum began to carry her, too, over the crumbling stone.

"Toni!"

His arms caught her and wrenched her back with almost inhuman strength. For a moment it seemed they would both go over, and Antonia could feel the shudder of the parapet as the old stones began to give way. But then, somehow, Richard dragged her from the edge and onto the relative safety of the balcony nearest the castle wall, where the deep drifts surrounded them.

The snow blew angrily around them, but Antonia was conscious of nothing except the loving safety of Richard's arms.

And the tragedy of two people destroyed by a twisted, evil woman.

Epilogue

"*H*ere it is." Sitting on the edge of the bed where Antonia was, at last, warm, Richard held the family history book open on his lap. He had been searching for a particular reference, and had finally located it.

"Who was she?" Antonia asked quietly.

He read in silence for a few moments, then looked up at her. His face was still somewhat drawn; Antonia's close call on the balcony had shaken him badly. But his voice was steady when he replied to her question.

"Her name was Miriam Taylor. She's included in the book only because she grew up in the castle, and because she was the ward of Parker's father. You were right—the author of this history had no idea she was responsible for what happened to Parker and Linette. Apparently, no one did. Linette must have taken that secret to her grave."

"And Miriam wouldn't have told anyone, even if she believed it was her fault." Remembering what she had seen, Antonia shuddered. "She was . . . sick, Richard. If you could have seen her in this room, what she did . . ."

"I didn't even see Linette in my room, not this time. It wasn't yet midnight, but I was about to come over here because I couldn't stand not being with you a moment longer. Then I heard you cry out. By the time I reached the hall, you were nearly at the widow's walk. And Parker was only a few steps behind you."

"You didn't see Miriam?"

"No. And, until you told me, I had no idea what had happened out there. All I saw was you."

His voice remained steady—now. But he had sworn at her frantically when he had carried her back to her room little more than half an hour ago. He had been too anxious over her shivering to be much interested in anything except getting her warm again. But once she was tucked into the bed and no longer so pale, he had heard the whole story from her.

Antonia fumbled one hand from beneath the covers and reached out to him, smiling when his fingers instantly closed over hers. "You saved my life," she said gravely.

His voice roughened. "Don't remind me of how nearly I came to losing you. Never, as long as I live, will I forget the terror I felt when I saw you hurtling toward that wall."

"I know it was foolish," she admitted. "But somehow I couldn't think of that. It was all so heartbreaking—and such a tragic waste for all of them. I wanted so badly to stop it, change it . . ."

"Yes, I know. But it happened, sweet. No one can change it now."

"If only Linette hadn't run. If only she had faced Parker and asked him to explain."

Richard hesitated, then spoke very deliberately. "If she had, Parker might not have died. But their love would have been changed forever by suspicion. It was, after all, his word against Miriam's that what Linette saw was a lie. He had no witness, no one to step forward and call her a liar. Linette might never have been able to forgive Parker. For his betrayal."

Antonia's grave eyes searched out his every feature as if she had never seen them before. She was still trying to reconcile two disparate men—and the only way she could do it was to accept the possibility that one of those men had been a lie, a creation.

Who was to say that a woman might not go to extremes in order to get—or keep—the man she wanted? Miriam had. And in so doing, she had caused Parker's death.

Claire Dalton might well have done all in her power to keep Richard Allerton for herself. She might have hired a thief to break into his house, out of greed or revenge because he had turned away from her. Finding the fob could have been pure chance, and since the button had been engraved with Antonia's initials, it would not have been difficult to figure out that Richard had fashioned himself a memento.

A woman might even have guessed how that button had come to be lost.

After all, what did Mrs. Dalton have to lose by her lies? If Richard really had ended their arrangement, she might have believed there was a chance he would return to her once his betrothed was out of the way—and she might have guessed that a young woman such as Antonia would likely break the engagement in a burst of emotion and flee. Richard might have returned to his mistress in anger.

There was really, Antonia realized suddenly, no other logical reason why Mrs. Dalton would have visited her, or said the things she had—except for spite or the desire to reclaim something she had lost. If her relationship with Richard had been as solid as she had said it was, she would never have jeopardized it by going to Antonia. The result, as anyone of reason might have guessed, had been scandal and a severe blow to Richard's pride—neither of which was a thing any man would thank his mistress for inviting into his life.

"Toni?"

She realized that she had been silent for a long time, and that he was watching her intently. "I have said a great deal about broken trust, haven't I?" she said. "But the truth is, if I had trusted you as I claimed to, I would have at least listened to your side of the story. I'm sorry, Richard. I should have listened—and I should have believed you."

"Do you believe me now?"

Antonia nodded, and the resistance inside her was gone as easily as that. She believed him because she loved him and accepted his honesty. And because, after what she had witnessed tonight, she knew the folly of trusting her own eyes and ears to tell her . . . all of the truth. Sometimes, only the heart could know that.

"Yes. I do believe you."

She went into his arms eagerly, pushing the bulky covers away so that she could feel the hard strength of his body against hers. He kissed her with intense desire, a little rough because the fear of having so nearly lost her was still with him, and she responded to his passion as she always had.

It was a long time later when Antonia lay close beside her duke in the warm bed. As sleep tugged at her, she thought of a question left unanswered. "Richard? In the book—does it say what happened to Miriam?"

He pulled her a bit closer and sighed, stroking

her tumbled hair. "Yes, it does. Six months after Parker's death, she threw herself from the widow's walk."

Antonia wasn't much surprised by the information, and gave it only fleeting attention. Her thoughts turned to Linette and Parker, and to their daughter Mercy. Perhaps those three had been doomed to short lives and anguish, but all of them had known love. And all of them refused to completely let go of life. Was that a testament to love? Tragedy? Family?

She didn't know. But she was deeply grateful that she had been given the opportunity to learn something from an old tragedy, and even more grateful that her own mistaken belief in betrayal had not demanded so high a price from the man she loved.

Unlike Linette, she had been given a second chance. And she intended to make the most of it.

"Merry Christmas, love," Richard said, pressing a tender kiss to her forehead.

Antonia had a flashing vision of future holidays filled with happiness, laughter, and the delighted cries of children. Perhaps, she thought, the sounds of life and love would fill this castle one day. She meant to make sure of that, because now the castle felt like home to her. Besides, she and Richard had a debt to repay. Perhaps only the contentment of their descendants would lay the restless spirits of the Wingate family to rest.

Perhaps.

Snuggling up to her betrothed, Antonia wondered sleepily how many Wingates had occupied this bed over the years, and if any of them might visit it from time to time. It would be unnerving to wake up with a ghost in one's bed. But Antonia wasn't particularly concerned about the possibility, and it seemed too much trouble to worry about—or to warn Richard.

"Merry Christmas, darling," she murmured.

KAY HOOPER is the award-winning author of *Hunting Fear, Chill of Fear, Touching Evil, Whisper of Evil, Sense of Evil, Once a Thief, Always a Thief,* the *Shadows trilogy,* and other novels. She lives in North Carolina, where she is at work on her next book.

Surrender

LISA KLEYPAS

To Patsy Kluck with love

Prologue

December 1875
Boston

"*C*ome on in," Hale said, throwing open the front door with a flourish. He gestured for Jason to precede him into the house.

Jason followed him into the entrance hall, appreciating the house's splendidly dark interior and quietly luxurious atmosphere. He raised his eyebrows and whistled silently.

"I'm glad to see you're properly impressed," Hale remarked with a grin. A dour-faced butler approached them, and Hale greeted him casually. "Hello, Higgins. I've brought a friend from college to stay for the holidays. Jason Moran, a fine fellow. Higgins, take our coats and tell me where my sister Laura—no, don't bother, I hear her singing in the parlor. C'mon, Moran." Hale strode past the staircase toward a room off the hallway. Jason followed obligingly, hearing a thin, girlish voice crooning "Deck the Halls."

A tall Christmas tree laden with ornaments and tiny wax tapers trembled in the center of the room. A slim adolescent girl in a blue velvet dress stood on a chair that was close to toppling over. She clutched an angel with glass wings in her small hand, rising on her toes in an effort to place it atop the tree. Jason started forward, but Hale was already there, snatching the girl by the waist and whirling her off the chair. "Here's my girl!"

"Hale!" she cried, throwing her arms around his neck and peppering his cheek with enthusiastic kisses. "Hale, you're home at last!"

"What were you doing up on that chair?"

"Putting the angel on the tree."

Hale held Laura's fragile body aloft as if she were a rag doll and inspected her thoroughly.

"You're prettier than she is. I think we'll put *you* up there instead."

She laughed and handed him the angel. "Here, you do it. And don't break her wings."

Instead of lowering Laura to the floor. Hale transferred her to Jason, who took her in a startled but automatic reaction. Afraid she might be dropped, she gasped with surprise and threw her arms around his neck. For a moment they stared at each other while Hale bounded onto the chair.

Jason found himself looking into a pair of soft green eyes fringed with dark lashes. He could have drowned in those eyes. Regretfully he saw that he was too old for her. He had just turned twenty, while she couldn't have been more than fourteen or fifteen. Her body was as light as a bird's, her breasts and hips not yet developed. But she was an exquisitely feminine creature with long chestnut hair that fell in curls down her back, and skin that looked as soft as rose petals.

"Who are you?" she asked, and Jason set her down with great care. He was strangely reluctant to let go of her.

"Ah, yes," Hale called down, in the midst of

fastening the angel to the prickly spruce branch, "introductions are in order. Miss Laura Prescott, may I present Mr. Jason Moran."

Jason took her hand, holding it as if he were afraid it might break. "I am pleased to make your acquaintance, Miss Prescott."

Laura smiled up at the tall, handsome man. He was making an obvious effort to speak carefully, but he couldn't hide the touch of a lilting brogue in his voice, the kind that housemaids and street peddlers and chimney sweeps had. His clothes were nice, and his black hair was thick and windswept. He was big and lean and healthy-looking, and his black eyes snapped with liveliness. "Are you from Harvard?" she asked.

"Yes, I'm in your brother's class." Realizing he was still holding her hand, Jason dropped it immediately.

"Moran is an Irish name, isn't it?" As Laura waited for an answer, she sensed his sudden wariness.

"Yes," Hale answered for him in a loud whisper. "He's Irish through and through."

Laura's smiled at her brother. "Does Mother know?" she whispered back.

"No, I thought we would let her discover it for herself."

Anticipating her narrow-minded mother's expression when she saw their Irish guest, Laura giggled softly and glanced at Jason. She saw that his black eyes had turned cool and unfathomable. Disconcerted, for she had not meant to give offense, she hastened to soothe him. "Mr. Moran," she said, "do forgive our teasing." She smiled, timidly placing her hand on his arm. "We always tease our friends."

For her it was a bold gesture, touching a man even in so impersonal a way. Jason could not know just how untoward it was. All he knew was that she was the most beautiful creature he had ever seen. Even in his ambitious dreams of being wealthy and having a fine home and a well-bred wife, he had not been able to imagine anything like her.

She was an aristocrat by birth, while he would never amount to more than a peasant in the Prescotts' estimation. For someone like him it was the highest honor just to be allowed to sit at their table. No matter how rich or important he became, he would never have a chance of marrying a Boston Brahmin. But he had beaten impossible odds many times before. Silently he vowed that he would do it again. When it came time to marry, Laura Prescott was exactly what he wanted.

It would take time and careful planning. Jason never counted on luck, which had always been in short supply in the Moran family. To hell with luck—all he had ever needed were his own resources. He did not return Laura's smile. In no way would he betray the thought that seared across his brain ... that someday she was going to be his.

One

November 1880
Boston

The last thing Jason Moran expected when he opened the door of his library was the sight of his wife being kissed by another man. Perhaps someone else's wife would resort to clandestine meetings, but not his. There were no secrets to Laura . . . or so he had thought. His black eyes narrowed while the unfamiliar sensation of jealousy froze the pit of his stomach.

The pair sprang apart as soon as the door opened. The light Strauss music from the party drifted in, dispelling any illusion of privacy the two might have had. Laura raised her hands to her cheeks in surprise, but that did not conceal the fact that she had been crying.

Jason broke the silence in a mocking voice. "You're not being an attentive hostess, darling. Some of the guests have been asking for you."

Laura smoothed her chestnut-brown hair and composed herself with miraculous speed, assuming her usual emotionless mask. "Don't look so anxious, Perry," she said to the other man, who had flushed scarlet. "Jason understands a kiss between friends." Her green eyes flickered in her husband's direction. "Don't you, Jason?"

"Oh, I understand all about . . . friends," Jason replied, leaning his shoulder against the doorway. He had never looked as dangerous as he did in that moment, his black eyes as hard and bright as diamonds. "Perhaps your friend will be kind enough to allow us some privacy, Laura."

That was all the prompting Perry Whitton needed to make his escape. Mumbling something apologetic, he skittered through the doorway, pulling at his high starched collar as if to relieve the rush of blood to his face.

"Whitton," Jason mused, closing the door behind the retreating figure. "Not the most obvious choice for a romantic liaison, is he?"

Perry Whitton was a shy, middle-aged bachelor, a friend of some of the most influential women in Boston society. He had innumerable female acquaintances, but never showed a romantic interest in any of them. Whitton's looks were pleasant but unthreatening, his manner engaging but not flirtatious. Any husband would feel completely secure in leaving his wife in Whitton's company.

"You know it was not like that," Laura said in a low voice.

Perry had been an acquaintance of the Prescotts for years—the kiss had been a gesture of sympathy not passion. As Laura had welcomed him to the party, Perry had seen the strain on her face and the unhappiness beneath her social pleasantries.

"You are as lovely as always," Perry had said kindly, "but I would presume to say that something is troubling you."

It was indeed. Laura had no intention of confiding in him about her problems with Jason, but to her horror she realized she was about to cry. She would rather have died than make an emotional scene. Understanding her dilemma, Perry had taken her to a private place. And before she could say a word, he had kissed her.

"Jason, surely you can't think there are romantic feelings between Perry and me," she said in guarded tones.

She quivered with unease as her husband approached her and seized her upper arms. "I own you," he said hoarsely. "Every inch of you." His eyes raked over the satin evening gown she wore. "Your face, your body, your every thought. The fact that I don't choose to partake of your favors does *not* mean I'll allow you to bestow them on any other man. You are mine, and mine alone."

Laura's astonished green eyes met his. "You are hurting me. Jason, you know the kiss meant nothing."

"No, I don't know that." He glanced down at her body in that insulting way again, his cruel gaze seeming to strip off her garments. "You're a beautiful woman, beautiful enough to make even Perry Whitton want you. He may have made the mistake of thinking he could find some warmth in that slender little body. Perhaps he isn't aware that you're as lovely and cold as a marble statue."

Laura flinched and turned her face away. Jason could see a moist patch on her cheek where her tears had not yet dried. He had never seen her cry, not in all the time they had known each other. "What were you crying about?" he demanded, his voice as rough as the blade of a saw.

Laura was silent, staring at him uncomprehendingly. In her family there had never been displays of anger or violence. Hale's boyish antics had provided the only excitement in the Prescotts' placid world. During the last years when her brother had been away at school, her life had been as quiet as a nun's. As Jason glared at her, demanding that she explain herself, she was too overwhelmed to speak.

Cursing savagely, Jason yanked her against him. Her racing heartbeat pounded against his, and her skirts flowed around his feet. His dark head bent, and his mouth crushed hers. She whimpered and tried to pull her head back, but he caught her jaw in his fingers and held her still. His lips were hard and bruising, his kiss infused with raw anger. She gasped and went rigid, enduring the brutal onslaught.

Jason let go of her so swiftly that she stumbled back a few steps. "I can feel how my touch disgusts you," he jeered. "It must be humiliating for the daughter of Cyril Prescott to be fondled by a grocer's son. You were meant to marry a Boston Brahmin, but instead you became the wife of a workingman, a shanty mick. I bought you, paid for you with money so new the ink was barely dry. I know how your friends pity you. God knows you have reason to pity yourself."

Laura's face turned white, the marks of his fingers showing on her jaw. They stared at each other in the brittle silence. When it became clear he was going to say no more, she turned and fled the room as if the devil were at her heels.

Jason dropped his black head and rubbed the back of his neck wearily. He was filled with self-hatred. He had promised himself he would never hurt her, and once again he had broken that vow. He had spent his entire life trying to overcome his heritage and hide his rough edges. Most of all he had devoted himself to making money, for he had realized in his youth that being rich was the only way to compensate for the lack of a proper name and bloodlines.

In the past two months of marriage, Laura had organized his life and provided for his comforts with an efficiency he would never take for granted. Managing the household, entertaining their friends and guests, and accompanying him to social events were things she did with ease. Her taste was flawless, and he didn't question her opinions even when it came to his own clothes. Subtly she influenced him in matters of style and discrimination, and he valued her advice.

Jason knew how other men envied him for his wife, and he took pride in her accomplishments. Laura co-sponsored charitable functions for the benefit of the poor and was a member of the Ladies' Christian Association. Her leisure pursuits were all proper and respectable: attending lectures, going to the theater, and encouraging the arts in Boston. Everyone agreed she was a quiet but charming woman, a model of self-restraint. Not for a minute did Jason regret marrying her.

But that did not make her contempt for him any easier to bear.

He remembered the day he had approached Cyril Prescott for Laura's hand in marriage. In spite of their distinguished name, the Prescotts' fortune was dwindling. Such "first families" sometimes found it necessary to sacrifice one of their daughters to the vulgar newly monied class. Marrying Laura had not been as difficult as Jason had expected. It had boiled down to a matter of money, and he had been easily able to meet Cyril Prescott's asking price. "I would not consent to this," Cyril had said, looking both indignant and shamefaced, "if I thought you would prove to be an unworthy husband to my daughter. But you appear to hold her in high regard. And there is obviously no question that you will provide well for her."

"She'll have everything she wants," Jason replied smoothly, concealing his triumph at finally obtaining the woman he had wanted for so many years. Afterward he had proposed to Laura in a businesslike manner, informing her of the decision that had already been made between him and her father. They never had a courtship—Jason had felt it would be unwise to give her an opportunity to spurn him, which she most certainly would have done. Instead he had maneuvered the situation so that she had no choice but to accept him as her husband. He knew there was no other way he could have had her. She was desired by every eligible man in Boston. Had it not been for him, she would have become the wife of a gentleman with blood as blue as her own.

In time, Jason had thought, she would learn to accept him . . . and then perhaps he could begin to reveal his feelings for her. Unfortunately he had not anticipated how repelled she would be by his touch. She had such obvious disgust for her socially inferior husband that, God help him, he—who had always been so self-contained—couldn't seem to stop himself from losing his temper around her.

Keeping her head down, Laura strode rapidly along the hallway, her only thought being to escape. A short distance away was the large music room, which also doubled as a ballroom. The crowd of guests indulged in light conversation and danced to the buoyant waltz being played by the orchestra. Oblivious to the music and laughter, Laura made her way through the entrance hall to the front door and slipped outside. The November air was damp as it bit through her brocaded satin gown. She shuddered in misery and wrapped her arms around her middle, staring out at the dimly lit street where lacquered broughams and liveried drivers waited for the guests to depart.

Drawing herself into the porch shadows of the fashionable six-story Beacon Street home, Laura wondered what she was going to do. It was obvious that Jason hated her. She could not face him anymore. She was a failure as a wife, as a woman. Tears welled up in her eyes, and she willed herself not to cry. Good Lord, what if someone saw her out here, weeping on the steps of her own home?

Suddenly she heard a cheerful whistle on the street. Anxiously she stared into the darkness. "H-hale?" she cried. "Hale, is that you?"

Her brother's gentle laugh drifted to her. "Hmmm . . . why, yes, I believe it is. Have I crossed the line between fashionably late and too, too late?"

Laura gave a watery chuckle. "As always."

"Ah, you'll forgive me," Hale said, and leaped

up the stairs with his customary vigor. "Have you been waiting for me? Damn, you're out here in that thin dress! How long—" He broke off as he took her face in his gloved hands and tilted it up.

Tears spilled from Laura's eyes, and she gripped his wrists tightly. "I'm glad you're here, Hale," she choked out.

"Laura, sweetheart." Alarmed, Hale pulled her head against the front of his wool coat. "My God, what's the matter?"

"I can't tell you."

"Oh, you can and you will. But not here." He ruffled her hair, carelessly disarranging her coiled chignon. "We'll go inside and have a talk."

Laura shook her head. "People . . . people will see—"

"We'll walk around the house and come in through the kitchen." Hale shrugged out of his coat and draped it over her narrow shoulders. "It has something to do with Jason, doesn't it?"

Her throat closed painfully, and she nodded. Without another word Hale put his arm around her waist and guided her down the steps, shielding her from the view of the drivers and passersby. By the time they reached the kitchen, which opened onto the backyard, Laura was shivering violently. The heat and light of the kitchen engulfed her, but they did not take away her numbness.

"Why, Mrs. Moran," she heard the housekeeper's voice exclaim.

Hale favored the older woman with an appealing smile. He had matured into a handsome and solidly built man with green eyes, rich brown hair, and a thick slash of a mustache. His openhearted manner charmed all women. "Mrs. Ramsey, I'm afraid my sister has the vapors," he said. "Could you find a way to inform Mr. Moran—discreetly, mind you—that she has retired for the evening?"

"Certainly, Mr. Prescott."

The vapors, Laura thought wryly. Well, it would work. The excuse was always accepted with quiet understanding. Because of the spoonbill corsets and heavy haircloth bustles worn under their gowns, women often experienced dizziness and fainting spells. In fact, such episodes were considered proof of a lady's refinement.

"Oh," Hale added as he guided Laura out of

the kitchen toward the stairs, "and would you have two toddies brought to the upstairs sitting room, Mrs. Ramsey?"

"Yes, Mr. Prescott."

Laura handed the coat back to Hale, and they began to climb the three flights of stairs to the sitting room. "You probably don't even know what the vapors are," she said with a sniffle.

He laughed. "No, and I really have no desire to find out."

They reached the sitting room. It was Laura's private place. No one intruded, not even Jason, unless she invited them. Like the other rooms in the house, it was comfortable and elegant, with a flowered Persian rug, velvet drapes, plush chairs, tiny polished tables covered with lace and ornaments, and a marble fireplace. Laura had chosen the carefully blended styles of furnishings for the entire house, all matters of taste being left to her discretion. Jason preferred it that way.

"Now," Hale said, sinking to his haunches in front of the fireplace, "tell me everything while I stir up the fire."

Laura gathered up the fringed train of her evening dress and sat in a nearby chair. Morosely she kicked off her damp satin slippers with their two-inch heels and tiny diamond buckles. It pleased Jason for his wife to be dressed in the finest of garments. "I don't know what to tell you," she said. "Jason would be furious if he knew—"

"Tell me everything," Hale repeated patiently, glancing at her over his shoulder. "Remember, I was Jason's closest friend until you married."

"Yes, I remember." Laura's mind turned back to all the holidays Jason had spent with her family. Although he and Hale had been in the same class at Harvard, Jason was two years older. He had never made pretensions about his background. His father had been a grocer, and his mother had peddled a fish cart.

It was highly unusual for someone of Jason's humble beginnings to have climbed as high as he already had. But Jason was intelligent, hardworking, and ruthlessly charming when he wished to be. Something in his voice and the way he moved proclaimed he was a man who knew exactly what he wanted—and what he wanted, he would get. And when he smiled, he was the most handsome man on earth.

"Laura, what's wrong?" Hale asked.

"Everything. It's been wrong since the beginning." She peeled her gloves off and wiped her stinging eyes. "Jason has no idea how overwhelming he is. I don't know how to please him, and when I try I fail miserably. I—I think something is wrong with me. Whenever we try to . . . be intimate, I don't do whatever it is he expects me to do, and—"

"Laura, wait." Hale cleared his throat uncomfortably, his cheekbones tinged with red. "If you're referring to the sort of thing that goes on in the bedroom, I think you had better discuss it with a woman."

Laura thought of her prudish mother and her straight-laced sisters. "Who do you suggest?" she asked.

Hale groaned and clutched his head in his hands, looking down at the flowered carpet. "All right," he said in a muffled voice. "Tell me. But keep in mind that a fellow doesn't like to hear about his sister and . . . that."

She shook her head. "There is nothing to tell you." After a brief pause, she repeated meaningfully, "Nothing."

Hale's astonished green eyes met hers. "Are you trying to tell me . . . my God . . . that you and Jason have never . . . *never*?"

"No," Laura said, embarrassed but strangely relieved to be telling someone.

Hale opened and closed his mouth several times before he could form another word. "Why not?" he finally managed to ask.

She held her head in her hands much as he had a moment before, while her words burst out in a swift torrent. "Jason has approached me a few times, but I—I make him so angry. The last time we argued he accused me of being cold, a-and I suppose I must be, but I can't seem to help myself! I thought that as time passed we might come to some kind of understanding, but things only worsened. He spends his days at his business offices, and he dines at his club, and whenever he is in the house we avoid meeting in the same room! There's not the least bit of trust or friendliness between us. The best we've been able to manage is politeness, but now even that seems to be beyond us."

"I see," Hale said, sounding strange. He stroked his mustache and shook his head.

"And tonight," Laura continued, "I was in the library with Perry Whitton, who kissed me—"

"He *what?*" Hale gave her a disapproving glance.

"Perry and I are friends, nothing more."

"All the same, Laura, you shouldn't have allowed it."

"It happened too quickly for me to say or do anything! And of course Jason walked in and misinterpreted the situation, and said that I must be ashamed of being the wife of a shanty mick . . . and I don't even know what that is!"

"That's what they call an Irishman, one from a peasant family so poor that even the women have to work." Hale sighed heavily. "A mick, a blackleg, a greenhorn. A few of the fellows at Harvard didn't give a damn about his being Irish, but most of them did. Jason was excluded and subtly insulted at almost every turn. After all, his background was the same as that of their servants. You know how they can be." He made a face. "Frankly, I can't blame Jason for being upset if he saw you with Perry Whitton. He is the epitome of all Jason could never be, a gentleman with the right name, the right family, the right upbringing."

Laura nodded in understanding. Boston society was fastidious about every entry in a family's genealogy. Change was regarded with suspicion, and everything depended upon who one's grandfather had happened to be. It was considered vulgar to work hard or make much money. The ideal Bostonian man was genteel, dignified, and intellectual. Someone like Jason, ambitious and driven, a self-made man, was a shock to the more refined Bostonians such as the Whittons.

"Hale," she said fervently, "if I had wanted a man of Perry's ilk, I wouldn't have married Jason. How can I make him understand that?"

"I don't know." Her brother looked guilty. "It won't be easy to convince him. Your entire family disapproves of his heritage. We all know that Father only consented to the betrothal because of the extraordinary amount of money Jason's made in real estate. And I . . . well, I told Jason at the beginning that I was against the marriage because he's Irish."

"Y-you couldn't have!" Laura exclaimed, horrified. "Hale, you don't really feel that way!"

"Oh, yes." He nodded stubbornly. "I explained to Jason that I valued him as a friend, but I couldn't approve of him marrying one of my sisters. Especially not you. I knew how difficult it would be for you, never quite belonging in one world or the other. I had known for a long time that Jason wanted to marry someone with a name, someone who could gain him entry into our circles. And—hell, I'll be frank—he comes from crude beginnings, Laura."

"That doesn't matter to me," Laura said, and cleared her throat awkwardly. "It has never mattered to me that Jason is Irish."

The maid knocked at the door and brought in their toddies on a small silver tray. Laura took the tray from her and dismissed her with a wan smile of thanks. She gave Hale his drink and sipped slowly on hers, welcoming its bracing effects.

"Well," Hale said, "let's address this business about this 'coldness' of yours. I'll wager some of this is Mother's influence."

"Hale, I can't blame her for—"

"Don't defend her, sweetheart. She raised all three of her daughters to believe that it is natural for a husband and wife to live as strangers. For years I knew about the ridiculous things she told you and Anne and Sophia, but it wasn't my place to contradict her." He sighed and regarded her sympathetically. "These matters are not complicated, Laura. It's very simple. All you have to do is show Jason that you're willing to accept his attentions, and he will take care of the rest of it. He is an experienced man. Just allow him to . . ." He stopped and began fiddling uneasily with the silk fringe of the brocaded chair. "He wouldn't be cruel to you, Laura, not in that way."

She clasped her hands together tightly. "I wish I could believe that. But I don't know what to think about him anymore. I find myself wondering why I married him."

"Well, why did you?" Hale demanded.

"Father wanted me to, and it was a help to the family."

"Father and the family be damned! You know he wouldn't have forced you to marry Jason. The wedding would never have taken place had you uttered one word of objection."

Laura bit her lip and nodded, ashamed. "Yes, you're right. I . . . the truth is, I was more than willing. I wanted to be a wife to Jason." She drew her legs up and tucked them beneath her. "Jason thinks he doesn't need anything from anyone. But I knew the first moment I met him that he needed someone like me, to help and comfort him, to bring some warmth into his life. I was so certain I could soften him, and bring out another side of him." She laughed shakily. "And instead he seems to be changing me into something I never wanted to be."

It was three hours later when Hale made his way downstairs and discovered that the last of the guests had departed. Sliding his hands in his pockets, he ambled through the ballroom, where the musicians were packing their instruments.

"Was it a success?" Hale inquired of the young lank-haired violinist.

"Quite lively for your kind of crowd," came the cheerful reply.

Hale grinned and wandered past a pair of Irish maids carrying trays of empty glasses. "Pardon, miss," he inquired of one of them, "where might Mr. Moran be? Retired for the evening? No? Ah, drinking in the library. I'm not surprised. Mr. Moran does have a taste for whiskey, doesn't he?"

Jason was sitting in a chair before the fire, holding a bottle of liquor loosely in his hand. His legs were stretched out, his head resting against the brocaded upholstery. His black evening coat had been discarded, while the sleeves of his starched white shirt were rolled up to the elbows. His eyes were half-slitted as he stared into the flames, while the firelight played over his raven hair. He did not move as Hale walked into the room and closed the door.

"Usquebaugh," Hale said, using a Gaelic word Jason had once taught him. He gestured casually toward the whiskey. "You micks call it the water of life, don't you?"

"Go to hell."

"Very likely." Hale dragged up a heavy chair with his foot and collapsed into it. "First, however, I'm going to have a talk with you."

"If you're half-witted enough to think I'm going to listen—"

"I believe I'll begin with a few observations." Green eyes met black, and they exchanged a long glance, the glance of adversaries who knew each other's secrets. "So far everything has gone according to your plan, hasn't it?" Hale said.

"Remember telling me about the plan years ago? Remember what you said?"

Jason arched a black eyebrow. "I said that by the time I was twenty-five I would have graduated from Harvard with honors."

"And established yourself in the Boston business community."

"Yes."

"And married a girl whose name would allow you into the most elite social circles."

"Yes."

Hale smiled ironically. "At the time, although I admired your ambition, I didn't believe you could do it. But you've accomplished all that. You married my own sister. You're being referred to in Boston as 'that damned Irish tycoon,' and by the time you reach thirty, you'll have multiplied your fortune several times over." He leaned forward, losing some of his flippancy as he demanded, "What, then, is the cause for bitterness? Why are you behaving like such a bastard to Laura, when you have everything you ever wanted out of life?"

Jason swished the whiskey in the bottle and stared into its swirling contents. He was tempted to confide in Hale, but he could not let go of the grudge between them.

"Don't answer, then," Hale said. "I already know why."

Jason's eyes gleamed dangerously. "You've always known all the answers, haven't you? A Prescott's prerogative."

Hale shrugged.

Jason extended the whiskey bottle with a scowl, and Hale took a drink without hesitation. "You've been talking with Laura," Jason said.

"Yes, and she's owned up to a few things I've been suspecting for some time."

"It's a dangerous game, prying into matters that have nothing to do with you."

"Nothing to do with me?" Hale exclaimed, his temper sparking. "Laura is my sister, my *favorite* sister, and you're making her miserable! Of all the girls in Boston you could have married and made miserable, why did it have to be her?"

Jason rested his forearms on his knees, a shock of black hair falling over his forehead. He answered slowly, watching the fire with a brooding gaze. "There weren't all that many girls to choose from. It had to be someone with a name, and someone with the qualities I wanted in a wife. And most of all it had to be someone whose family was in financial straits and had need of a rich son-in-law."

"So when it came time to marry, you cast your eyes around and there was my youngest sister—"

"I decided to marry Laura the first Christmas I spent with your family."

Hale frowned, the ends of his mustache curving downward. "That long ago?"

"Yes. Laura was only fifteen. When the family sat down to dinner I nearly made some excuse and left. I would rather have faced a firing line than confront that endless row of spoons and forks at each plate. I didn't know which one to pick up first, or how to eat the damned asparagus. And there was your mother, watching every move I made like a hawk. But Laura was slower and more painstaking than everyone else, and I was able to imitate everything she did. Halfway through the meal I realized she knew I was aping her. She was being slow and precise in order to make it easier for me."

"Hell, *I* never bothered with Mother's blasted rows of forks."

"You didn't have to," Jason said flatly. "You had nothing to prove."

"And so you decided to marry Laura because she helped you get through a meal?"

"Because I knew she would be the kind of wife I needed."

Laura had said much the same thing. Hale set down the bottle of whiskey and stood up, glaring at his former friend. "Ah. A house-keeper. A social companion. A teacher of etiquette. A pretty ornament to impress the hoi polloi. There were other girls you could have married if that was all you wanted. Laura has more to give than that, and she deserves more than to spend the rest of her life trying to make you into a gentleman."

Jason smiled nastily. "You think she's too good for an Irishman?"

"Not at all. I think she's too good for *you*."

Retrieving the whiskey bottle, Jason gestured toward the door. "Understood. Now get the hell out of here."

Hale paced around the room in frustration. "I've never seen Laura as high-strung and nervous as she was tonight. You're crushing all the fire and spirit out of her."

Jason stood up to face him. "*Fire* and *spirit*," he repeated sarcastically, thinking of his pale, poised wife, "are not words I would apply to your sister, Hale."

"Oh? Now I'm beginning to understand how little you really know her. She's the most adventurous, free-spirited girl I've ever . . . why, once on a dare she sneaked into Father's room and cut off half his mustache while he was sleeping. She loves swimming and skating and riding. She's a crack shot, a first-rate pianist, an excellent dancer. She's always dreamed of going to Egypt and seeing the pyramids, and traveling up the Nile in a *dahabeah*—"

"A what?"

"*Dahabeah*. One of those long boats."

Jason stared at him with narrowed eyes. "Hale, I don't know who the hell you're talking about, but it isn't my wife."

"It damn well is! And there's something else you should hear—"

"I've heard enough."

"Falling-out or not, I should have talked to you before the wedding about Laura. This notion you both seem to have—this supposed coldness of hers—"

"Out," Jason said tersely, herding him toward the door.

Hale talked rapidly. "Dammit, Jason, you obviously haven't realized how sheltered she's been. My other two sisters had a devil of a time adjusting to marriage after the way they'd been reared. If Mother were a Catholic, she'd consider the *convent* too permissive for her daughters. Most girls have opportunities to flirt and hold hands with men, enjoy a stolen kiss or two. My sisters had none of that. As you know, Jason, I have a great deal of respect for my mother—but there's no denying that she's a bitter woman. My father has been unfaithful to her, not once but many times. My parents' marriage went sour long before Laura was even born. Laura's been brought up with some mistaken ideas about men and women, and by God, you've probably confirmed every last one of them! All because you seem to expect her to hop into your arms like some barmaid!"

"The lecture is over," Jason snapped, kicking the door open with the side of his foot.

"*Listen*, damn you! Before she married you, Laura had never been alone with a man before, not for a minute. She's not cold, she's an innocent, a complete innocent who doesn't even know how to kiss. She's always been shy around men, especially those with a tendency to be overbearing. And all you do, all you've *ever* done, is frighten and accuse her! How is she supposed to be responsive to you?"

Jason's hands dropped to his sides, and his black eyes fastened onto Hale's agitated face.

"If you treat her with just a little patience or kindness you might be able to make her happy," Hale said in a cutting voice. "I've seen you with women. I've seen you seduce the most hard-hearted of them inside of a quarter hour. But for some reason all your renowned charm seems to vanish when it comes to Laura." He tugged his own sleeves down and straightened his coat lapels. "You've been married for two months, and so far all you've done is build a mountain of misunderstandings. You and I may no longer be friends, Jason, but for Laura's sake and your own, I hope you give some thought to what I've said." Turning away, Hale walked to the front hall, snatched up his greatcoat, and left without a backward glance.

Jason stared after him, his brows drawn together in a frown. Slowly he went to the stairs and sat down, raking his hands through his disheveled hair. He thought of his wife in bed, clad in one of her demure white gowns, her long hair braided loosely, her skin flushed with sleep. He had gone in there countless nights to watch her while she slept, being careful never to awaken her. The sight of her never failed to arouse him unbearably.

When Laura was awake, however, her green eyes seemed to say what everyone else did, that Jason was unworthy of her, that Cyril Prescott's daughter should never have married so far beneath her. But . . . what if that expression in her eyes was not disdain? What if it was something else entirely? Was it possible that he had made his own wife afraid of him?

Cursing, Jason thought over the past weeks and counted the scant number of times he had been gentle with Laura—God, no, he had been too busy dwelling on her resentment of him. As much as Jason hated to admit it, Hale had been right about something. There were misunderstandings that had to be cleared away, for both their sakes.

* * *

Laura's cup rattled in its saucer as Jason's broad shoulders filled the doorway of the breakfast room. Hastily she set the saucer down and lowered her gaze to the linen tablecloth. The silence was agonizing. Should she say something? Something accusing, something appeasing. Words of forgiveness? . . . reproach? Perhaps—

"Laura."

His voice was quiet and serious. Blankly she looked up at him, her eyes shadowed from a sleepless night.

Jason was struck by how young she looked, silhouetted against the white lace curtains at the window. Her chestnut hair was pulled into a coiled braid at the nape of her neck and tied with velvet ribbons. The pointed basque of her chocolate-brown dress was buttoned high up to her throat, the sleeves long and puffed at the tops. In spite of the strain evident on her delicate features, she was as lovely as always.

Jason could not stop his gaze from flickering to the curve of her breasts molded beneath the tight-fitting bodice, and the flash of white throat above the tiny lace collar. Quickly he looked away before she could read his overwhelming desire. He wanted her desperately. It would have been a simple matter to find release with another woman, but Laura was the only one he wanted. Perhaps, he thought cynically, it was a just punishment for his past sins, being married to a woman who was revolted by his touch.

"Jason," Laura said, gathering up her courage. "After last night, I—"

"No," he interrupted. "Let me speak first."

She fell silent in confusion. There was an expression on Jason's face she had never seen before, earnest and uncomfortable. The way his eyes searched hers caused a wave of heat to rise from her neck to her face.

"I'm sorry for what I said—and did—last night," Jason said in a low voice. "I was angry. I wanted to hurt you."

Unconsciously she raised her fingers to her throat. "You did," she replied softly.

"It will not happen again."

Laura had never been so surprised, not even the day he had proposed to her. She heard herself murmuring something, but the voice did not seem to belong to her. "This is the f-first time you've ever apologized to me."

Jason smiled at that, his eyes alight with self-mockery. "It may be the first time I've ever apologized to anyone. I've always thought of it as a sign of weakness I couldn't afford."

Laura did not know if she was more relieved or astonished by his oddly agreeable manner. "Will you have some breakfast?" she asked, trying to hide her nervousness.

"No." Jason ventured further into the room, lean and handsome in his tailored black coat, gray trousers, and quietly patterned vest. As he came close to her, she rose from her chair and backed away a step or two. He appeared not to notice her involuntary movement. "I have a great deal of business to attend to this morning," he said. "And I'll be home late tonight." A brief hesitation followed before he added, "I thought that tomorrow morning we would leave to spend the rest of the week at your sister's home in Brookline."

"Brookline? But your work—"

"The world won't come to an end if I stop working for a few days."

Laura was astounded. For as long as she had known him, Jason had been obsessed with his work. "We have never accepted Sophia's invitations before," she said. "Why would you want to spend time with my family when you've made it clear—"

"Yes, I know what I've made clear—and what I haven't." He took another step toward her, and she skittered back once more. "Laura," he said gently, capturing her wrist with ease. He held her hand so lightly that she could have pulled away with little effort. "If you would rather not go to Brookline . . ."

"Oh, no, I—I think it would be a fine idea."

His thumb slipped into her palm and lingered in the soft hollow, and she felt the sensation of his caress all the way down to her knees.

"Good," he murmured.

They were standing close enough for her to detect the scent of his cologne. She felt him looking down at her, and in vain she waited for him to release her hand. But he waited patiently as well, making no move to let go. After long seconds dragged by she raised her head.

"You haven't said you'll forgive me," he re-marked.

"I—I do."

His thumb still played idly in her palm, and she knew that he could not help but be aware of her agitation. Slowly, easily, his free arm slid around her. Laura endured the closeness for a few seconds before a natural reflex caused her to break free of him with a sound of protest. Horrified, she retreated to the side of the room, certain he would jeer at her. She waited for a rebuke that never came. Instead there was silence.

Jason approached her with the smoothness of a panther, not stopping until she was flattened against the wall and he was just inches away. He rested one forearm over her head, his body looming over hers. For an instant she recalled how it had felt to be crushed against that hard body.

"Laura . . ." His voice was husky. His hand slid to the back of her neck and tilted her face toward him. "In the past two months you've guided me in many things. And in spite of my display last night, you've even managed to teach me a few manners. But now . . ." Before she could move, he brushed his lips across her forehead. "Now there are some things I'd like to teach you."

Nervous chills ran down Laura's spine. She could not deny him. It was a wife's duty to submit to her husband's embrace, no matter how much she dreaded the prospect. "Whatever you wish," she said emotionlessly, her nerves writhing in turmoil.

A smile pulled the corner of his lips at her dutiful answer. "What I wish for is a kiss from my wife."

Laura searched his midnight eyes for mockery, and found an oddly challenging gleam. He expected her to refuse, she thought. She would show him that she was not afraid of him. Only a kiss . . . it was not such a dreadful request.

She held her breath and summoned all her courage, standing on her toes to accommodate the difference in their heights. Gingerly she pressed her lips to his, her palms falling to his shoulders for balance. To her surprise, the closeness was not unpleasant. His mouth was warm against hers, his shoulders hard and steady underneath her hands. He did not crush her in his arms or frighten her as he had so many times before.

Red-faced and trembling, she ended the kiss and sank to her heels, beginning to breathe again. But it appeared Jason was not through with her. His dark head bent, and his lips drifted over her temple, the curve of her cheek, the tiny hollow behind her earlobe. Laura's hands clenched into fists against his shoulders.

He slid his hands over her silky hair, pushing her head back. He took his time with her, noting that although she was not responding to him, she was not rejecting him either. Gently he brushed her lips with his own. She kissed like a child, her mouth innocently closed. Jason realized that the sexual urges so familiar to him were only just awakening in her.

The tip of his tongue traced her lower lip, lingering at the center. Laura jerked away from him in surprise, touching her fingers to the damp surface. Why had he done that? Was it wrong for her to allow it?

Jason's eyes held her in a dark, velvet prison. Carefully he pulled her back against his body. "It's all right," he murmured, his breath mingling with hers. "It's all right, Laura . . . did I frighten you?"

"No," she said faintly.

He smoothed her hair and kissed her temple, careful to keep every movement slow and gentle. "Would you put your arms around my neck?"

She hesitated and then obeyed, her breasts resting against his chest. The warmth of his hands cupped her jaws, holding her head still, and his lips teased hers with fleeting touches. "Kiss me back," he whispered.

Laura felt light-headed, her fear dissolving in a wave of slow, sensual curiosity. She relaxed in his arms, her lips no longer closed so firmly, accepting the gently playful mouth that moved over hers. The tip of his tongue ventured further and further, probing until she opened her mouth with a gasp. She felt his tongue begin a languid search for hers, stroking deep in a way she had never dreamed of.

Eventually he lifted his mouth, and she realized dazedly that she did not want the kiss to end. She rested her head on his shoulder, soothed by the long, repeated strokes of his hand along her spine. His palms pressed her buttocks and hips forward until there was not an inch of space between their bodies. They were separated by the thick layers of her skirts and petticoats, but even so she could feel the hard ridge of his loins.

Jason held her close between his thighs, allowing her to become accustomed to the feel of a man's body. His lips wandered over her moist forehead, while the uneven gusts of her breath against his neck caused his manhood to swell even more blatantly. He felt her trembling as he fondled the downy nape of her neck. "Afraid?" he asked.

"I . . . I don't know."

"There's nothing to be afraid of." He rubbed his lips over hers in a roughly teasing caress. When she did not respond, he raised his head and looked at her questioningly.

Her eyes were luminous and turquoise-green, while her kiss-reddened lips were softer and fuller than usual. Wonderingly she lifted her hand to smooth back the hair that had fallen over his forehead.

Suddenly they were interrupted by the opening of the door to the kitchen. It was Phoebe, a housemaid who had been in the Prescott's employ for nearly ten years. Phoebe's round face turned the color of raspberries, and her mouth fell open at the sight of husband and wife clasped together in the breakfast room. "Oh, my. Ex-excuse me," she exclaimed in horror, and disappeared behind the door.

Laura tried to smooth her hair and dress, while her skin burned with embarrassment.

"We are married," Jason reminded her dryly,

tightening his arms around her back.

"You should let me go—"

"Not yet. Is it so unpleasant to be held by me?"

"I would not like anyone else t-to break in upon us again." She closed her eyes as she felt him nuzzling her ear.

"If you would prefer some privacy," he said in a soft voice that raised every hair on the back of her neck, "we could go upstairs."

She tried to pull away from him. "I—I have many things to do today if we are to leave for Brookline so soon. I do think you should let me go—"

"Then go, if you're so damned eager to fly out of my arms." He released her with a slight scowl. But his tone was far more gentle than usual, and she felt his gaze caressing her as she turned away. "Laura."

She stopped without looking at him. "Yes?"

"I am not going to force you to do anything," he said quietly. "I have wanted you for a long time, and I haven't yet forced you."

He was more overwhelming in his gentleness than he had ever been in anger. Laura was astonished by the feelings that swept over her: the desire to walk back to him and press herself against his body, to slide her fingers through his coal-black hair, to feel his mouth on hers again. She left the room quickly, her heart pounding with the knowledge that in less than a few minutes her husband had turned her entire world upside down.

Two

A fresh snow had covered the ground, giving the rebuilt farmhouse a picturesque appearance. As the driver opened the door of the double brougham, a burst of icy air swept away Laura's pleasant lethargy. The drive from Boston with Jason had been surprisingly enjoyable. In response to her questions, he had talked to her about his construction enterprise in the Back Bay, an apartment building of twenty-five flats complete with elevators and steam heating.

"I would like to see it," Laura had remarked, and he regarded her with a skeptical smile.

"I'll take you there when we return."

Laura nodded in assent, while her insides quivered in delight. Jason had never been so nice to her. She began to think that the next few days might not be as harrowing as she had feared. Since their marriage, they had never spent longer than an afternoon with her family. When any of the Prescotts were near, Jason was quiet and abrupt, his manner challenging. The Prescotts, in turn, were stiff and polite. Laura always felt caught between two opposing forces, and she was miserable when they were all together. But if everyone made an effort to be pleasant, it might pave the way for future gatherings.

Jason stepped out of the carriage and reached up for her, catching her around the waist. Laura pulled her hands from her tiny fur muff and grasped his shoulders. He swung her down without letting her feet touch the portable steps.

"Thank you," she said with a breathless laugh.

His dark eyes studied hers, and he smiled ruefully. "A house full of Prescotts," he said, keeping his hands on her waist. "I feel as if I'm about to brave a lion's den."

"You got on well enough with them before we were married," Laura pointed out.

Suddenly he grinned. "Yes, until I made you a Moran." Still holding her, he looked over her head at the large house, surrounding fields, and wooded copses. Well in the distance was the outline of the Boston State House dome, and the tall buildings near it.

The Prescotts often gathered at Sophia's Brookline home during the winter. The first-born of Cyril Prescott's children, Sophia was a plain but sociable woman. She had a talent for entertaining, and it was universally agreed that Sophia was one of the most accomplished hostesses in Boston. Her husband, Judge T. Horace Marsh, was a rather stiff-necked blue blood, but Sophia's influence had caused him to soften during the past few years.

Sophia was one of the rare breed of Bostonian women who liked to dispense with unnecessary formality. In her home the younger people were allowed the free use of first names, a custom which irked the older generations. No one was allowed to remain a stranger in the Marshes' gatherings. They were all cajoled into joining the constant rounds of whist and backgammon, sleigh rides and dancing parties.

Sophia appeared on the landing of the outside steps, her lips curved in a welcoming smile. She was clad in a stylish winter dress of gray cashmere and garnet velvet. "My dears, how wonderful to have you here at last," she said, pressing Jason's hand between hers, then embracing Laura. "Come inside at once. We have a splendid fire, and hot tea for the ladies, and something stronger for the gentlemen. Anne and Howard are here, and so are the Warrens— oh, and Jason, you'll be pleased to learn that Hale arrived not an hour ago." Sophia inclined her head toward them confidentially. "I believe Hale is seriously thinking of courting the Warrens' daughter Prudence. I told him that the two of you might not be averse to chaperoning them on the sleigh ride this afternoon."

Laura and Jason exchanged a questioning glance, and Jason replied while holding his wife's gaze. "Of course I'll chaperone Hale," he said, a little too nicely. Laura suppressed a laugh, pitying her brother.

Jason guided her into the house with his arm

at her back, pulling her to the side as the servants moved past them to carry their trunks upstairs. Slowly Jason untied the laces of Laura's velvet-trimmed mantle. She was unable to look at him as she felt his fingers at her throat.

Jason handed the garment to the waiting arms of a maid, and glanced over Laura's head to his sister-in-law. "I wouldn't mind a glass of the 'something stronger' you mentioned, Sophia."

"I suggest you join Hale and the other men in the parlor," Sophia replied. "They are congregated around a bowl of hot punch, discussing whatever it is men discuss amongst themselves." She slipped an arm around Laura's shoulders and smiled. "We sisters must confer with Cook about the dinner preparations."

Jason's black eyes glinted with amusement. "Certainly," he said, and although his voice was bland, it was obvious he knew they were planning to gossip.

Together Sophia and Laura watched his broad-shouldered form as he left, then they wandered toward the kitchen. "Now, out with it," Sophia said. "How did you manage to drag Jason here?"

"It was his decision," Laura replied. "No one is more surprised than I."

"Hale confided to me that he had a talk with Jason, but he would not reveal what was said between them."

Laura frowned darkly. "I will not have Hale interfering in my marriage, no matter how well-intentioned he is. I will speak to him about it."

"Oh, don't be cross with him! You know how Hale adores you. He cannot bear to see you unhappy." Sophia peered at her younger sister. "*Are* you unhappy? Jason is not being unkind to you, is he?"

"Not at all." Laura folded her arms in a stubborn gesture.

"Hmmm. The two of you look well enough. And Jason is as wickedly handsome as ever. If it were not for his regrettable background, he would have been the prize catch of Boston." With studied casualness, Sophia added, "But of course there will always be those who say you must be pitied for marrying a shanty-born Irishman. No one would blame you for feeling ashamed."

"Why should I be ashamed of a man who has lifted himself from poverty to prosperity? Jason has had to fight for everything he's ever had. Nothing has been given to him. Nothing has been easy for him. He is a man of intelligence and strength. I'm *not* ashamed of him, yet for some reason Jason finds that as difficult to believe as everyone else!"

There was a gleam of satisfaction in Sophia's eyes. "Then you must persist until you do convince him. It is a woman's duty to make the best of her lot, Laura. And there are *certain things* a wife owes to her husband."

Laura turned red up to her hairline at Sophia's delicate emphasis on 'certain things.' "Hale told you everything, didn't he?" she asked, feeling betrayed.

"I won't deny it."

"I should have known I couldn't trust him to keep my confidence."

"Hale felt you would benefit from the advice of an older sister," Sophia said implacably. "You and Anne and I were not given an adequate education in how to be good wives. We learned all of the practical things and none of the truly necessary things. We never learned about trust and affection, and most of all loyalty. Father's philandering embittered Mother years ago. She never wished for her daughters to risk the danger of loving a man and perhaps being hurt by him."

Laura regarded her speculatively. "I wouldn't have expected such frankness from you, Sophia."

"I have discovered many things in the past few years. I have learned to love my Horace, and not to withhold myself from him." She raised her eyebrows slightly. "I suspect that Jason has not been the shining example of a devoted husband. But a good wife could make him into a good husband. *If* he's as intelligent as you claim. And the best revenge, my dear, against those who would mock or pity you for your common red-blooded husband, is simply to be happy."

What seemed to be at least a dozen children ran and cavorted around the four sleighs lined up in front of the house. Some of them were Sophia's offspring, others belonged to the Warrens, and the remainder were distant Prescott cousins. Laura stopped at the top of the circular steps with Prudence Warren, a vivacious and friendly girl she had met once or twice before.

"How lovely the sleighs are," Prudence exclaimed, and Laura agreed. Each vehicle with its shiny black runners was pulled by two horses with festive tassels and bells affixed to their harnesses. A driver in a top hat sat at the front of each sleigh. Laughing young men and women were piling into the sleighs and covering themselves with wool and fur blankets, while others were helping the children clamber aboard.

"Now I can believe Christmas is only three weeks away," Prudence said.

Laura looked at her with a faint smile. "Are you and my brother planning to exchange gifts?" she could not resist asking.

"That depends on Hale," Prudence said airily. "If he gives me something proper and acceptable—candy or a book are all Mama will allow—then I shall give him something in return."

The two of them watched as Hale stomped toward the last sleigh with two giggling children under his arms, loudly demanding that someone relieve him of his burden. Jason walked around to him, reached for the children one at a time, and settled them into the vehicle. The little boy reached for the ends of Hale's mustache and refused to let go, causing Jason to laugh. The scene reminded Laura of the days when her husband and brother had been close friends, and she smiled wistfully. It was good to see them being civil to each other. She could not help but hope that they might someday regain their closeness.

"Your husband is quite charming," Prudence said, following her gaze. "And good with the children."

He was, Laura saw with a touch of surprise. Expertly Jason separated a pair of quarreling siblings, rescued a tot who was wandering close to the horses' hooves, and carried a little boy on his back from one sleigh to another. While Jason organized the group and conferred with the drivers, Hale bounded up the circular steps to Laura and Prudence.

"Laura, sweetheart," he said cheerfully, grasping her small gloved hands.

Remembering the way he had confided her private affairs to her sister, Laura pulled her hands from his and gave him a frosty glare. "I've had a revealing talk with Sophia," she said.

He looked sheepish, but didn't bother to pretend he didn't understand. "I'm sorry."

"I didn't give you permission to tell anyone about Jason and me."

"Sophia hit upon it with some damned clever guesses, and hang it, I couldn't lie to her."

"You could have said nothing," Laura said coolly.

"But with Sophia that's the same as admitting everything! Sweetheart, don't get all ruffled, there's a—"

"I have a right to be ruffled, you traitor." Laura folded her arms over her chest and turned away.

Swearing under his breath, Hale regarded her guiltily and then offered his arm to Prudence.

"Hale, whatever is—" Prudence began, but he interrupted her with a scowl.

"Don't ask, Pru. With three sisters, a fellow's always in one stew or another." He walked Prudence down the steps, while Jason passed by them on the way up.

Jason raised an eyebrow as he looked from Hale's face to Laura's. He smiled at the sight of his wife dressed in a smart sleighing costume of black satin and brocade, and a lynx-trimmed mantle. A tiny black bonnet trimmed with red ribbons and ostrich plumes was perched on her head. Every hair was in place, every ribbon and pleat perfectly arranged. Jason wanted to scoop her up and kiss her right there on the steps.

Laura's glare faded immediately as she saw him. He was especially handsome today, his black hair smoothly brushed, his wool overcoat tailored to his broad-shouldered form. "I was coming to find you," he said, sliding his hands over her ribs, his thumbs resting just underneath her breasts.

She held onto his arms, her green eyes shyly meeting his. "It is quite a large sleighing party," she said.

"Yes, and we're the only married couple of the group. I hope we can keep all of them in order."

"I have no doubt of it." She used her mittened hand to whisk away the snow that clung to his shoulder. "A horde of Prescotts should provide no difficulty for you."

Jason tilted his head and regarded her with a slow, quizzical smile that made her heart turn over. "We'll see if your faith is justified." He kept his arm around her as he helped her down the steps. "We're riding in the last sleigh to keep all the others in sight."

He lifted her into the sleigh and strode to the front of the line of vehicles, where the first driver awaited the signal to go. Slowly the sleighs began to move. Laura sat opposite Hale and Prudence, while Sophia's four children were bundled between them. The youngest, a seven-year-old girl named Millicent, crept into Laura's lap and huddled under the woolen robe.

Jason came to join them, climbing into the empty space beside Laura. Together they arranged the blankets, the child, and their tangled legs, until Laura began to laugh. Finally she was tucked securely against Jason's side, her leg wedged against his muscled thigh, her head near his shoulder. Disregarding Hale and Prudence's interested gazes, she leaned against him.

Millicent sat up in Laura's lap, asking questions about the horses, the trees, and anything else that struck her fancy. Jason answered her patiently, reaching out to tug one of the little girl's long brown curls. The deep murmur of his voice was at once soothing and exciting to

Laura, flavored with the hint of a brogue that would never quite disappear. She listened to him and watched the sparkling scenery around them, the frozen ponds and snow-laden birch and pine that lined the sleighs' path.

The group in the lead sleigh began singing, and gradually the tune was picked up by the entire line of vehicles. Laura joined in with the others, smiling at Hale's enthusiastic rendition.

Over the river and through the wood,
To grandfather's house we go;
The horse knows the way to carry the sleigh,
Through the white and drifted snow . . .

Observing Hale and Prudence together, Laura decided her brother was truly smitten with her. She glanced at Jason to see if he had noticed Hale's unusual behavior. Jason read her thoughts exactly. He bent his head and whispered to her. "I expect your father would approve of a match between the Prescotts and the Warrens."

"Not entirely," she whispered back. "The Warrens are rich in respectability but poor in common sense. Their family fortune has shrunk to almost nothing. And Father has always wished for Hale to marry a girl with an impressive dowry."

"Hale could try working." They were both aware that Hale's position at a Boston bank was little more than a sham, designed to protect the Prescotts' interests. The genteel occupation was common among young men of Hale's position in society. It would have been slightly vulgar for him to be seen actively working to accumulate wealth, as if he were one of the immigrant nouveaus.

"A Prescott?" she asked doubtfully.

Jason grinned. "Not easy to imagine, I'll admit."

Hale interrupted them indignantly. "Here now, what are you two whispering about? I feel my ears burning!"

Before Laura could reply, the line of sleighs came to a stop. Jason half-rose from the seat and stared far ahead of them, using a gloved hand to shield his eyes from the glare of the snow. "Looks like a tree limb blocking the path," he said, jumping down. "I'll be back in a moment."

"I'll lend a hand," Hale said, and leapt after him.

Laura and Prudence were left with the curious, excited children. Wilfred, Sophia's small and bespectacled ten-year-old son, gazed at the inviting drifts of snow. "Aunt Laura, can I get out? Just for a minute?"

"I don't think that would be a good idea," she said cautiously. "I'm certain we'll be under way at any moment."

"Just for a minute," Wilfred wheedled, and Millicent took up the plea.

"Aunt Laura, can I go with him? Please, Aunt Laura—"

"I don't think—" Laura began, and Wilfred interrupted.

"Why, the others are all getting out!" the boy said hotly. "And they're . . . why, they're throwing snow b—"

Prudence shrieked as a soft white clump of snow flew past her ear. Suddenly the air was filled with happy shrieks and pelting snowballs. Wilfred leapt out of the sleigh and scampered to a nearby tree, scooping up a handful of fluffy snow on the way.

Laura set Millicent aside and stumbled after the boy. "Wilfred! Children, all of you behave! There is no—" She ducked with a gasp as a snowball came flying toward her and landed on the ground behind her. "Who threw that?" she demanded, trying to sound authoritative. The scene was chaos, men and women ducking and throwing, children screaming with delight.

Laura burst into laughter, running as fast as she was able to the protection of her own tree. Leaning against it, she tore off her mittens and began packing her own snowball. She felt like a little girl again, free and uninhibited.

Jason made his way back to the last sleigh, keeping his head low. The vehicle was empty. He looked around quickly, wondering where the hell his wife had gone. It was certain that she was not participating in this free-for-all— she was probably hiding somewhere until it was over.

"Look here, Moran!" Hale's voice came from far ahead of him, and Jason turned quickly enough to evade a hurtling snowball. Jason returned the fire, hitting Hale squarely in the chest. Hale clutched the white splotch of snow on his coat and keeled over clownishly, causing a multitude of children to yelp happily and fall on top of him.

Jason chuckled and began to stride toward

the squirming pile of youngsters. Suddenly he felt a solid *thump* between his shoulder blades. Spinning around in surprise, he saw the flap of a black cloak from behind a tree. His eyebrows drew together. Laura? No, his timid, docile wife would not have dared. Another snowball hurtled toward him, and he avoided it deftly, his eyes narrowed in curiosity. He saw a pair of discarded mittens on the ground. "Laura?" he said, perplexed.

His wife peeked at him from behind the tree, the plume on her hat dancing. Her eyes sparkled with merriment, but there was also an alert quality in her expression. It was clear that she had no idea if he would lose his temper or not.

With an effort Jason cleared the astonishment from his face. He felt a smile twitching at his mouth. "So you want to play . . ." He reached down to scoop up a handful of snow and began to stalk her.

Understanding what he intended, Laura shrieked and fled, gasping with laughter. "No, Jason! Remember, I'm your wife!"

Her skirts slowed her down, but she darted among the trees, venturing deeper into the woods. Hastily she flung clumps of snow behind her. She felt a small *thwack* on her posterior. His aim was deadly. "I surrender!" she called out, her voice quivering with laughter. "Jason, I surrender *wholeheartedly*!"

But Jason was nowhere to be seen. "Where are you?" she called, turning in circles. "I admit defeat!" She packed a snowball together as quickly as possible, in case he refused to be a gracious victor. "Jason?" There was a crunch of ice behind her. Whirling around, she saw Jason just before he pounced on her. She gave a short scream and tried to hit him with the snow, only to send them both falling to the plush white-blanketed ground.

Jason twisted to cushion the fall with his own body, then rolled over, pressing Laura into the snow. His husky laughter mingled with her giggles, and he raised himself on his elbows to stare into her face. "Surrendering wholeheartedly," he said, "means laying down your weapons."

"I didn't have a white flag to wave."

"Your aim is good," he said.

"You make a large target."

He grinned and picked up a large fistful of snow, brandishing it threateningly.

"I've already surrendered!" she squeaked, covering her face with her wet hands.

He dropped the snow and pulled her hands away, keeping hold of her wrists.

Her smile faded as she stared at his dark face and felt the weight of him between her thighs. He stopped smiling at the same instant, his gaze falling to her lips. She remembered the way he had kissed her in the breakfast room— the hot, wet interior of his mouth, the urgent hardness of his body. He was going to kiss her again . . .

"Has the tree limb been taken care of?" she asked.

"Yes. We should be leaving soon." Jason drank in the sight of her flushed cheeks, her half-closed eyes, the crystal-white puffs of her breath in the air. He wanted to take her right here, in the cold and the snow, wanted to sink into her slim, exquisite body and feel her mouth open and sweet underneath his.

He loosened his gloves finger by finger and pulled them off. With one fingertip he stroked a damp tendril of hair off her forehead. "Are you cold?" he murmured.

She shook her head blindly. The cloak kept

her insulated from the dampness of the snow, and the length of her body pressed to his felt as if it was glowing with heat. His fingertips moved over the sides of her face like points of fire, trailing to her jaw and tilting her chin up. His breath was like steam against her skin.

She lifted her icy-wet fingers to his face, timidly exploring the line of his cheekbones, the tips of his slanting eyebrows. His head angled over hers, and his lips nudged hers in a velvet-soft kiss. With a small sound of pleasure, she slid her arms around his neck, and then the glittering white world around them seemed to fade away. He brushed another savoring kiss over her mouth, and then another, until her lips parted and she unconsciously pulled at his neck to bring his mouth harder against hers.

He gave it to her as strongly as she wanted it, allowing his hunger to dictate the movements of his lips, his tongue. Her slim fingers combed through his midnight-black hair and kneaded the back of his neck. Deliberately he tightened his knees on her thighs, and she arched into his body with astonishing fervor. The fact that she was responding to him at last made him as shaky as a boy with his first woman. The frightening truth was that he needed her as he had never needed anyone. She was his, and she alone could take away the loneliness and nameless hunger he had felt ever since he could remember. She was his, and he wanted her to acknowledge it with her body and her heart.

"Laura," he said, burying his mouth in her neck. "Laura—"

Hale's drawling voice was a shock to both of them. "You two are the most disgraceful pair of chaperones I've ever seen."

Laura started at the intrusion. Her eyes flew open and she tried to struggle wildly to a sitting position. The skirts and petticoats tangled around her legs, weighting her down.

"Easy—it's only Hale," Jason said, filling his lungs with a deep breath of cold air.

"Don't let him tease," she whispered, clutching the front of his coat. "Not about this."

"No," Jason said soothingly. "I'll kill him if he tries." He stood up and reached down for her. She took his hands and allowed him to pull her upright. Then she was utterly still, her crimson face averted as he reached around her to brush the snow from her cloak.

Hale regarded them both with a self-satisfied

smile. His mustache twitched like a cat's whiskers. "A nice respectable married couple," he continued mischievously, "should be doing their utmost to preserve order and propriety, and instead I find you here rolling in the snow like some—"

"Enough, Hale," Jason said curtly.

He looked surprised. "Why, Laura, you aren't *embarrassed*, are you? I'm your brother, and besides—"

"Hale," Jason said in a voice of warning, and even Laura felt her spine tingle at the sound of it.

Hale sobered immediately. "The others are climbing back into the sleighs. I came to find you before your absence became widely noticed."

Jason regarded him sardonically. "Thanks."

"No thanks necessary," Hale said, and gestured for them to accompany him. "I'll go back with you."

"No." Jason shook his head, pulling Laura's unresisting form closer to his. "Go on ahead. We'll be there soon."

"Don't take long." Hale looked at Jason over Laura's head, gave him a brilliant smile, and raised his hand in the gesture of a victorious prizefighter.

Jason scowled at him and pointed threateningly toward the sleighs. Hale left with all due haste.

Laura, who had missed the exchange, wedged her arms against Jason's chest to keep from being too close to him. She couldn't think when she was near him. He straightened her hat and pulled out the broken red plume, handing it to her apologetically. She accepted the bedraggled feather and looked at Jason with dismay.

"I've never seen such a blush," he said huskily, and hugged her to him.

Her arms crept around his back. "Shouldn't I blush?" she asked, her voice muffled in the front of his coat.

"Not with me." He kissed her forehead, and she shivered at the masculine scrape of his jaw.

Laura could not fathom the reason for his sudden tenderness. Perhaps he had decided to play some sort of game with her. "Jason," she said bravely, "things cannot change between us, not in the course of a few days."

"Yes, they can." His thumb stroked the side of her neck, lingering at her pulse. "For the past two months I've let my pride stand in the way of what I really wanted. That's going to change. We know as little about each other as we did on our wedding day. And that"—he kissed the side of her throat—"is damn well going to change."

Laura was silent and troubled, wanting suddenly to cry. It was all happening too fast. How could she give herself to him when she knew all too well that he could turn cruel in one capricious moment?

Jason read her expression and experienced the taste of bitter regret. She was so young, and he had hurt her in ways he had not understood until now. "I won't hurt you, Laura," he said quietly. "Not anymore. And I'll have your trust no matter what it takes."

The evening was filled with games, amusing stories, and music at the piano. After dinner the guests gathered in the parlor, which originally had been two smaller rooms which Sophia had converted into one large one. Laura sat with Sophia and a group of married women while they laughed and discussed the latest happenings in Boston. The unmarried girls had formed their own group a short distance away, while the men congregated around the fireplace or puffed on cigars in Judge Marsh's smoking room down the hall.

Laura could not keep her eyes from her husband. As usual, Jason was dominating the group in his own charismatic way. What he lacked in sophistication he made up for with the spark of irreverence that was quintessentially Irish. Jason never seemed to be bored except when confronted by a particularly starchy Bostonian, and then he was capable of saying or doing something just outrageous enough to make everyone laugh. Because he made no pretenses about his background, no one guessed at his sensitivity about it. He was fully aware that there were many who enjoyed the appearance of friendship with him, but few who would have tolerated the idea of him marrying into their families.

Toward the end of the evening Laura noticed that Jason had become quieter than usual, his gaze frequently diverted toward her. She could feel him staring at her, and when she looked back there was an intent gleam in his eyes that made her flustered. She nervously declined when Sophia pushed her to play the piano, but her older sister was insistent.

"Do play something for us, Laura. Something lively."

"I can't. I'm sadly out of practice," Laura said.

"But why? You used to play all the time before . . ." Sophia stopped, but Laura knew she had been about to say *before you married Jason.*

Laura stiffened as she felt Jason's hand at her back. "Play something," he said quietly.

She felt a spark of indignation at what sounded very much like an order. She knew that Jason liked to show off his accomplished wife—he wanted her to play for the same reason he dressed her in fine clothes and jewels. Well, if he was determined to put her on display, he could share the limelight!

She turned her head to regard him challengingly. "If you turn the pages for me."

His dark gaze did not waver from hers. "All right."

"Splendid," Sophia exclaimed, rifling through pieces of music to find what she wanted. "It's a pity you cannot play, Jason, otherwise I would choose something you could do together. I suspect you never had the patience for lessons, hmmm?"

He smiled. He did not point out that pianos and music lessons had not been a great concern for a family that had scratched and clawed for every penny. "Page-turning is one of my more underappreciated talents," he said, guiding his wife to the piano bench and helping her sit. He arranged the music in front of her. "Now, Laura," he said silkily, and she knew he was enjoying her annoyance, "when it is time for me to turn, just nod your head."

She glared at him discreetly. "I'd rather kick your leg."

One corner of his mouth lifted in a half-smile. "You're full of surprises today," he said. "I'm beginning to wonder if my Irish temper hasn't rubbed off on you."

She began to enjoy being pert with him. "My temper is entirely my own."

"I didn't know Bostonians had tempers."

"They do," she said crisply. "The slow-burning kind."

"Better to let out their anger at once and have done with it."

"I doubt you'd enjoy having a wife who gave

233

vent to explosions of temper whenever she felt inclined."

"You're wrong," Jason said, resting his weight on one leg and draping his forearm on the piano. A lock of black hair fell over his forehead as he stared down at her. "I'd enjoy having her very much."

Laura's cheeks turned apple-red. She touched her fingers to the keys and tried desperately to remember how to play. There was no possibility of getting through the piece without making countless blunders. Not when he was near—not when he was in the same *room* with her.

But somehow her hands moved, recalling the sprightly melody with ease, and she did not falter. His lean fingers turned the pages at just the right pace. And all the time she was so terribly aware of him. When he leaned close enough that his shoulder brushed hers, she felt an unfamiliar ache in her breasts.

She finished the piece with a short sigh of relief and graciously accepted compliments from Sophia and the others. Jason helped her up, his hand strong at her elbow, and someone else took her place at the piano.

"Well done," he said.

"Thank you." Laura wished he would take his hand from her arm. She could not help remembering what had happened earlier today, the weight of his body pressing hers into the snow, his demanding mouth teaching her things she had been innocent of.

"Why don't you play for me at home?" he asked.

"Because I don't wish to," she said bluntly.

He scowled, drawing her to the side, away from the others' observation. "Why the hell not?"

"Jason, your language—"

"Tell me why not."

Recklessly she cast aside her fear of his temper and told him. "Because I would not like having to perform at your command, whenever you wish to be entertained, or whenever we have guests you wish me to play for like some. . . . some trained monkey!"

"Dammit, Laura," he said softly, "I won't be blamed for depriving you of something you enjoy. If you don't feel like playing when I want you to, tell me to go to hell."

In spite of their quiet tones, the tension between them was perfectly apparent. Laura sensed the glances being directed their way, and she straightened her spine until it resembled a fireplace poker. "I won't be drawn into public arguments with you," she whispered sharply. "That may be done where you come from, but it's not done in Boston society!"

"It's done all the time in the North End," Jason said, relaxing a little, sliding his hands into his pockets. "And my grandparents thrived on it in County Wexford. Perhaps we should give it a try once in a while."

She looked scandalized. "Jason, the very idea—"

"I'll buy you an iron skillet to threaten me with. That will lend us a touch of authenticity."

In the midst of her anger Laura felt a smile tugging at her lips. "I do not want a skillet. And I do not want to play for you."

Jason looked at her with those disturbing black eyes, and although they were in a room filled with people, she felt as if they were alone.

As the hour grew late the guests became drowsy. They began to retire, the ladies gliding to their rooms, where maids waited to assist with the removal of bustles, petticoats, and corsets, and the brushing-out of intricate coiffures. Laura walked upstairs with Sophia while Jason remained with the men, who lingered over cigars, brandies, and unfinished conversations.

"Things seem to be going rather well," Sophia remarked as they neared Laura's room.

"You're referring to the guests?" Laura asked cautiously.

"Two in particular," came the airy reply. Sophia stopped and pressed her cheek to Laura's. "Good night, dear."

"Good night," Laura replied ruefully, and went to her room, where a small, cheerful fire was burning in the grate. The bedroom was decorated in bright floral chintz patterns of coral and green, the windows draped with cream lace curtains. A light netted canopy hung over the old high-post bedstead. But what most attracted her eye was the masculine trunk in the corner of the room, opened to reveal her husband's possessions.

She and Jason would be sharing the room. Laura remained still, while inside she felt a flurry of panic. Foolishly she had not considered the possibility until this moment. Of course they would be expected to share a bed . . . there were so many guests, and Sophia barely had enough rooms for all of them.

"Missus Moran?" The maid's quiet voice broke through her scattered thoughts. "Would ye like me to help wi' yer dress now, or—"

"Yes, do," Laura said, still staring at the trunk. She hardly felt the tugs at the hard-to-reach fastenings that trailed down the back of her gown.

Jason would want to stay the night with her. From the way he had been behaving lately, she had no doubt of that. But he had claimed he would not force her. If she pleaded with him to keep his distance, what would he do? Certainly he would be angry, but she did not think he would hurt her.

But *would* she ask him to leave? A mixture of fear and excitement nearly made her dizzy. What if she let it happen? What had Hale said . . . these matters were simple . . . just show Jason she was willing to accept his attentions.

Am I willing? she thought to herself. She could find no clear answer. It was up to Jason. If he approached her in a kind manner, if she could just let herself believe that he would not mock or hurt her, she would be willing.

She dressed in a white nightrail embellished with hundreds of tiny ruffles and tucks, the long sleeves and bodice ornamented with frothy lace. The white cambric wrapper she wore over the nightrail was even more elaborate, bordered with three deep lace ruffles at the hem and more lace from the wrists to the elbows.

Deciding to attend to her hair without assistance, Laura dismissed the maid with a smile of thanks. She sat at the walnut-veneered dressing table and stared into the small tilted looking glass. One by one she pulled the pins from her hair until the tangled chestnut waves fell down her back. Brushing it would take a long time, and the task was soothing in its monotony.

Laura was nearly finished with her hair when she heard a rap on the door, and her husband entered without waiting for permission. Their eyes met in the looking glass, his very dark, hers wide and green. Slowly she set the brush down. Still watching her, Jason pulled off his green-and-black-patterned waistcoat and narrow black necktie, and tossed them onto a chair.

The silence was heavy between them, the tension deepening until Laura could not bear it. With an incoherent murmur, she jerked up from the chair and strode rapidly to the door. She didn't know where she was headed, she only knew that she could not stay there alone with him another moment.

Jason caught her easily, his arm wrapping around her waist. He pulled her quaking form against his. "No, don't," he whispered against her ear, his hand sliding under her hair. His palm stroked up and down her narrow back.

"Not now. Please, not tonight," she managed to say.

"It all started with that damned wedding night," he murmured, fondling the back of her neck. "It was all my fault."

"No." She swallowed and shifted against him, and his hold tightened. "I behaved like a child," she ventured. "I—I turned you away."

"I didn't understand why, not at the time."

"I was . . . you were . . ." She flushed, overwhelmed by the memory . . .

Their wedding day had been long and nervewracking and tiresome, and by the time they had retired for the night Laura was exhausted.

Jason had been emotionless and matter-of-fact throughout the wedding and reception, and she wondered if he had any feelings for her at all. After allowing her time to change into her nightgown, he appeared in her room with his shoulders squared as if for an unpleasant duty. Since that was precisely what her mother had informed her was soon to follow—an unpleasant duty—Laura regarded her husband with a mixture of reluctance and alarm.

Jason had never looked as tall and overpoweringly large as he did in that moment. In order to hide her fear, she kept silent and looked away from him, her heart thumping violently as she heard the sound of his breathing. He slid one hand behind her head and the other around her rigid back. His warm, hard mouth pressed against hers for a long time, and she squeezed her eyes shut, her body frozen with confusion. She knew that something was wrong, felt that he wanted something from her that she was not able to give. His hand moved over her back and then to her breast. It was when he touched her there that she pushed him away in a quick, nervous movement. "Don't," she said without thinking.

His eyes narrowed in anger, as if he had been

expecting the rejection. "You'll have to get used to the idea of being my wife," he said, and reached for her again.

This time his mouth was hurtful, and his hand roamed over her body with insulting boldness. She tolerated it for as long as she could before jerking away with a tearful plea. "Don't touch me, I can't bear it!"

He looked as though she had slapped him. She covered her face with her hands, her whole body shaking. It was with relief and horror that she had heard him walk out of the room and slam the door . . .

The episode had been repeated a few times since then, until Jason had not approached her anymore. Until tonight.

"You were so strong," Laura whispered, "and you wanted so much. Things I didn't understand . . . things I still don't understand. I know now that you didn't intend to frighten me, but you did. There was such a look in your eyes . . ." She took a trembling breath.

It was fortunate she did not look up, for the same expression was in Jason's eyes right then, a hot glow of hunger.

"I didn't realize how innocent you were," he

said, raising his hand to her head, stroking her flowing hair. "The mistake was mine. I was too damned impatient for you. When you stiffened and pulled away from me, I thought it was disgust you were feeling, not fear."

"Disgust?" she echoed in bewilderment.

"Because you knew I was so far beneath you. Because you'd been forced into marriage with someone whose ancestors were nothing but peasants in the poorest country in Europe. I knew what everyone had been telling you, that I was not fit to touch—"

"No!" Impulsively she covered his mouth with her fingers. "I was not forced into marrying you," she said in astonishment. "Did you think I had no choice?"

His blank look was her answer.

"Oh, Jason, my father gave me every opportunity to refuse your proposal! Didn't you know that?" She smiled tremulously as she saw the shock on his face. Had he been so accustomed to prejudice from others that he had expected it of his own wife? "No wonder you made those remarks about buying me! But I was more than willing to marry you. The decision was mine to make."

Jason pulled Laura's hand away from his lips. "You don't have to say that."

"I'm not lying, Jason. It's the truth."

He shook his head stubbornly. "I made the bargain with your father before I proposed to you."

"And you thought he would have made such a bargain without my consent? You thought I was merely a pawn with no say of my own?"

He scowled at her. "Yes."

"You were wrong," she said with a touch of impatience. "I *wanted* to marry you. For heaven's sake, I've wanted to be your wife since I was fifteen years old!"

Suddenly Laura realized what she had said, and she covered her mouth with her hand. The bald declaration seemed to echo in the small room. *Don't let him ask why*, she thought frantically, *please don't let him ask why*.

Mercifully he didn't.

But he stared at her strangely, his black eyes seeming to read her most private thoughts. Blindly she lowered her head, and was confronted with the broad, shirt-covered expanse of his chest. He spoke softly, his mouth against her hair. "I want to set aside the past, Laura. I want to share a bed with you tonight." The tip of his finger traced the delicate edge of her ear, causing her to shiver. "Most of all, I want you to trust me to be gentle with you."

She had imagined and dreaded this moment for so long. Jason had never been this way with her before, so tender and careful. The choice of surrender was suddenly made easy. Tears sprang to her eyes. "I don't know what to do," she faltered.

"I'll show you."

Three

Deftly his fingers moved among the buttons and bows of Laura's wrapper until the garment slipped from her shoulders. Jason pushed the white cambric down her arms and over her wrists. She stood before him in her nightgown, her soft body unconstricted by stays and laces. He settled his hands on the natural curve of her waist, his senses enthralled by the scent and nearness of her.

Little by little he sank his hands into her loose hair until he was cradling her scalp. He bent his head and covered her mouth with his. Laura shivered at the masculine brandy-taste of him.

The tip of his tongue coaxed her lips to part, and he kissed her as if he would never have enough, his hands easing her head back. Swaying dizzily, she reached for his waist to keep her knees from buckling. He wrapped his arms around her until her breasts flattened against his hard chest and her thighs were leaning into his. Her mouth twisted wildly, her tongue seeking his, her slim body molded to him like a second skin.

They broke the kiss at the same time, gasping roughly. Laura took advantage of his loosened arms and stepped back, clasping her hands to the center of her chest. Her heart thundered in a way she thought he must be able to hear. She glanced from Jason's flushed face to the thrusting outline at the front of his trousers. Hastily she looked away, but not before he had seen.

"Curious? Here, come closer." He drew her forward, tender and predatory. "Don't be afraid."

"No, Jason, I don't—" She stumbled against him, and he caught one of her hands, bringing it to his groin.

Heat radiated through the cloth of his trousers, seeming to scorch her hand. She blushed and tried to pull away. He covered her hand with his own and kept it pressed against his rigid flesh.

"Have you ever seen what a man looks like?" he murmured among the wisps of hair at her temple.

She turned her hot face into his shoulder, shaking her head.

"Never spied on Hale and his friends taking a swim, or—"

"No, never." She gave a choked laugh, still hiding her face.

A teasing note entered his voice. "You were a proper little girl." Slowly he let go of her hand. Her fingers remained against him for a scant second, then withdrew to the safer territory of his waist.

"My mother made certain that all of her daughters were proper."

"She wanted to keep you sheltered from men," he said without asking.

"Well, she . . . has never had a good opinion of them."

"Because of your father."

"Yes." Laura stared at him curiously. "Hale must have told you about that."

"Why don't you tell me?"

"My father is a good man, a kind one. But . . . there have always been other women. Sometimes his involvements are merely flirtations. Sometimes they are more than that." She shrugged helplessly. "He has always been discreet, but Mother has known for years. She says it's to be expected that a man will be faithful to a wife for only so long. She says that most husbands will stray because . . ." Abruptly Laura fell silent.

"Go on."

"I don't think—"

"Tell me."

She obeyed reluctantly. "Because they are creatures of a bestial nature." Her green eyes met his. "Mother also said that you were probably more bestial than most."

Jason grinned, knowing that of all the people who had disapproved of their marriage, Wilhemina had objected the most. "Her opinion of my character has never been a secret." He became serious, lifting her chin with his fingers. "Do you believe what she said about unfaithful husbands?"

Her gaze skidded away from his. "I don't know."

His voice was very quiet. "Do you think I've been unfaithful to you?"

Startled, she looked up at him. Her mouth went dry. "Things have not been right between us," she managed to whisper. "You've had cause to be."

There was a flash of something vibrant, perhaps anger, in his eyes. But his hand was still gentle on her chin. "By now you should know me well enough to be certain of a few things," he said, his gaze boring into hers. "I never lie. When I make a promise, I keep it." Laura wanted to shrink away, but she was mesmerized by his intensity. "I took you as my wife because I wanted you and no one else. I made a vow to forsake all others. It's been hell going to bed alone, knowing you were just a few doors away. More than once I thought about going to you and taking what was already mine."

"Why didn't you?" she whispered faintly.

"Pride. That and the desire for you to open your arms to me willingly." His smile had a self-mocking quality that made her uneasy. "And so I've waited. And since the day we were married I've been planning my revenge for all the times I couldn't have you."

Laura turned pale at his quiet tone. "What . . . what kind of revenge?"

He drew closer, his hard-planed face serious, his mouth nearly touching hers. "I'm going to give you such pleasure that you'll weep for each and every night we could have had together." He picked her up and carried her to the bed.

The firelight spread its wavering glow throughout the room as Jason lowered Laura to the mattress and stripped back the covers. Ferociously he tore off his shirt and bent over her, his hands framing her face as he kissed her. Instinctively she adjusted her mouth to his, answering the sweep of his tongue with delicate touches of her own.

Curiously she touched the hair on his chest, trailing her fingers through the thick, springy mass. She found a thin line of silken hair arrowing down to the waist of his trousers, and she rubbed the back of her knuckle across it in a questioning touch. To her surprise, she felt Jason's breathing turn ragged.

He growled low in his throat and sought the peak of her breast through the bodice of her nightgown. Finding the hardening tip with his mouth, he nibbled gently. Laura gave a startled cry and twisted away from him, holding her hand to her breast.

"Did I hurt you?" he asked huskily.

Her cheeks pinkened, and she shook her head.

He pulled her protective hand away, replacing it with his own, his thumb circling the throbbing nipple. As he caressed her, he stared into her eyes, watching the green depths soften with pleasure. "You're so beautiful, Laura . . . I want to see the rest of you."

She didn't make a sound while he untied the bodice and took hold of the hem to draw it up her legs. She pressed her knees together modestly, feeling the cool air sweep over her legs . . . hips . . . waist . . . chest. Casting the garment aside, Jason gathered her slender body against his. When he pulled his head back to look at her, there was an absorbed expression on his face that she had never seen before. For him, too, time was suspended, and the outside world had disappeared. His kiss was relentless, flavored with desperation as he sought to make her understand how much he wanted her. Laura clasped her arms around his neck and sank her fingers into his black hair.

With a muffled groan, Jason let go of her just long enough to shed the last of his clothes. He pulled her to the mattress with him and slid his hands over her body with incredible gentleness. Her gaze wandered over him, and for a moment she couldn't breathe as she saw his naked, fully aroused body, primitive and golden in the firelight. Pinning her between his muscled arms, he lowered his head to her breasts. He covered the point of her nipple, his tongue gliding wetly across the aching bud. "Do you like it when I kiss you here?" he murmured.

"Yes . . . oh, yes . . ."

His mouth swept over her breasts, and he used only the lightest touches of his teeth and tongue. Wonderingly he stroked the length of her neck, the vulnerable hollow between her breasts, the downy smoothness of her stomach. Laura explored his body with the same sensitive lightness, bashfully touching the hair under his arms, the lines of his ribs, the lean surface of his flanks.

His palm ventured over her knees, his fingers tracing the line between her thighs. Her legs were still clenched together, resisting as he insinuated his hand between them. "Laura," he muttered, and she understood what he wanted. She felt the power and urgency contained in his body, the turgid length of him burning against her hip. "Laura, open to me."

She closed her eyes tightly and parted her knees enough to allow the gliding pressure of his hand. Jason kissed her breasts, her throat, whispering that she was safe, that he would take care of her. His lips brushed against hers, coaxing them apart, and his tongue reached for hers in skillful enticement that sent every hint of fear spinning out of reach.

His fingertips trailed over her stomach and dipped into the hollow of her navel. He paused at the triangle of soft chestnut hair at the top of her thighs, playing lightly through the curling strands. She began to breathe hard as his fingers slid deeper between her legs, stroking and withdrawing. Biting her lips, she tried to hold back a moan.

In spite of the desire that raged within him, Jason smiled triumphantly at the dazed, almost unwilling pleasure on Laura's face. He had brought that look to her eyes. He was the only man who would ever know her intimately.

Watching her closely, he slid his teasing fingers inside her. She groaned with pleasure, her hands climbing up his back.

Although her caresses were unskilled, they stirred Jason to violent readiness. Wanting her too much to wait any longer, he pushed her thighs wider and lowered his body between them. He felt her tense, and he cupped her head in his hands, his lips brushing against hers. "Sweet darling . . . easy now, *mo stoir*. It will hurt, but only for tonight." He positioned himself and pressed forward, gritting his teeth with the effort to be careful.

Laura clung to him, moaning his name as he sheathed himself within her. There was pain, a white-hot burning that caused tears to spring to her eyes. She writhed and tried to push him away, but he rode her movements easily. His lips drifted through the tear tracks on her face. "Easy," he whispered. *"Gradh mo chroidhe . . .* you belong to me now."

She began to relax as he cradled her in his arms, the hard force of him buried inside her. His mouth moved to her breasts, pulling gently on her aching nipples. Her heartbeat roared in her ears, and her lips parted as she breathed his name. He slid deeper within her, his hands beginning a slow sojourn over her body. The steady thrust of his hips brought pain, but she felt an urge to push up against him, and the sensation was intensely sweet.

His body surged into hers, pulled back until he had almost withdrawn completely, then surged forward again. Laura gasped as she felt the inner tension increase. Her muscles tightened, and she gripped his upper arms until her fingers were numb. Half-frightened by the unfamiliar sensations, she tried to draw back from them, but it was too late. A burst of pleasure filled her body, causing her to strain against him with an incoherent sob. Jason smothered her cries with his mouth and pressed deep within her until her shuddering ceased and she was satiated and quiet beneath him. Only then did he release his own desire, thrusting one last time and groaning with violent satisfaction.

Laura was too exhausted to move or speak. Jason rolled to his side and pulled her with him. It took the last of her strength to lift her arm around his waist. For a long time they lay with their bodies entangled and their breath mingling.

Jason was the first to speak. "You'll never occupy a bed without me again, Laura Moran," he said lazily. His fingers brushed away the tendrils of hair that clung to her forehead and cheeks.

A shy smile stole over her face. "Jason?" she asked, shivering as he cupped her breast in his warm hand.

"Mmmm?"

"What did those words mean?"

"Which words?"

"The Gaelic words you were saying . . . before. It sounded something like . . ." She paused and wrinkled her brow thoughtfully. *"Masthore.* And then you said something like *gramma-cree."*

Jason was frowning. "Did I say that to you?"

"Yes." She looked at him expectantly. "What does it mean?" To her amazement, she saw a flush of color that went across his cheekbones and the bridge of his nose. "Jason?"

"It means nothing," he muttered. "Just . . . words of affection."

"But what *exactly*—"

He kissed her, and as he had intended, the question flew from her mind. "You're the most beautiful woman I've ever known," he said against her lips as his hands wandered from her breasts to her thighs. "I'm going to give you everything you've ever dreamed of."

She laughed unsteadily, for Jason had never said anything of the kind to her before. All at once he seemed younger, the usual harshness of his face softening in the darkness, his smile almost boyish. "There's nothing I want," she told him.

"A golden carriage, drawn by horses with diamond bridles," he mused, rolling to his back and swinging her above him.

Laura crossed her arms modestly over her breasts. Her long hair hung in a curtain around her. "That isn't necessary."

"Ruby rings for your toes ... a castle with silver towers, a ship with moonlight sails to carry you across the sea—"

"Yes," she said. "I'll take the ship."

"Where would you like to go?"

"Everywhere."

Jason laced his fingers behind her neck.

"Would ordinary sails do? We'll travel anywhere you wish—perhaps spend a few months in Europe. Or the Orient." He raised his brows suggestively. "Or the Mediterranean."

Laura stared at him in wonder. "Jason, you're not teasing, are you?"

"I'm being serious. We never took a wedding trip."

"You said you couldn't afford to leave your work."

"I can afford it now," he said dryly. "Where would you like to go?"

"Cairo," she said with dawning excitement. "I've always wanted to see the pyramids."

"And make an excursion up the Nile?"

She blinked in surprise. "How did you . . ." She frowned suspiciously. "Is there anything Hale *hasn't* told you?"

Jason chuckled. "No. But that's the last of your brother's meddling. And you have my promise for a trip in the spring."

A sweet smile curved her lips. "Thank you, Jason."

He stared at her as if spellbound. "You can thank me another way."

"How?"

He took hold of her wrists and pulled them away from her body, his gaze lingering appreciatively on her round breasts before moving back to her face. "Lean down and kiss me."

She complied without hesitation, flattening her hands on his shoulders, lightly touching her lips to his. Beneath her she felt his body respond, desire flowing hot in his loins. Her eyes widened, and she tried to move away. He rolled to his side and slid his thigh between hers.

"Again?" she asked breathlessly.

"Again." His lips drifted over her neck in a moist, searing path. He murmured sweet beguilements in her ear, teased and fondled her until she was gasping and reaching for him hungrily. Laughing softly at her impatience, Jason slowed the pace even more, touching her as if she were as fragile as an orchid, as if more than the tenderest brush of his fingers would bruise her. He drove her past eagerness, past all reason, until all she could do was wait helplessly for him to release her from the silken prison. At last he slid into her, and she purred in exquisite relief, her green eyes half-closing.

Jason shuddered as he felt her arms closing around his back, her hips tilting to cradle his. He had never expected to find such fulfillment. All the bitterness, all the unspoken longings that had haunted him for so long, were quenched in the sweetness of her body.

The urgent rhythm of her hips pulled him into a flowing tide of pleasure, and he fought to keep his movements slow and easy. Laura muffled her moans of ecstasy against his shoulder, and Jason felt the shattering sensations sweep through him as well. He buried his face in the river of her hair, wrapped her in the shelter of his arms, held her tightly in the moments of darkness and bliss.

"Laura, dear. Laura." Sophia's voice called her from sleep.

She groaned, her face half-buried in the goose-down pillow. She squinted at her older sister, who stood by the bed. Sophia wore a velvet gown with an elegant knee scarf, a sash tied around the lower length of the skirt to gather it in at the knees. The curtains at the windows were tied back, letting in the white winter sunshine.

"What time is it?" Laura asked in a sleep-roughened voice.

"Eight o'clock, dear. I thought it best to wake you rather than allow you to sleep until a scandalous hour and become the subject of embarrassing speculation."

Laura began to sit up, then gathered the sheet to her breasts with a gasp as she realized she was naked. She blushed, throwing a cautious glance at her sister. Sophia seemed unperturbed.

"Is Jason downstairs?" Laura asked timidly.

"No, the men breakfasted early and went to hunt fowl," Sophia said.

"They went *hunting*?" Laura frowned in a befuddled way.

"The charm of the sport escapes me. I doubt they'll find a single thing to shoot. But after observing Horace's habits for years, I've come to the conclusion that men simply like to carry their guns through the woods, drink from their hunting flasks, and exchange ribald stories."

Laura tried to smile, but a quick, anxious frown followed. "How did Jason look at breakfast?" she asked.

"No different than usual, I suppose." Sophia's clear brown eyes rested on her steadily. "How should he have looked?"

"I don't know," Laura murmured, sitting up in bed. She winced, feeling battered and sore in every part of her body.

"I'll tell the maid to draw a hot bath for you," Sophia said considerately. "And I'll send up some cambric tea."

"Thank you." Laura continued to clutch the sheet closely, her fists winding and twisting in the soft linen. Sophia left, and Laura stared at the closed door, struggling with a mixture of emotions. "Oh, Jason," she whispered, distressed at the prospect of seeing him this morning. In the light of day, the recollection of her behavior was mortifying—she had been shameless, foolish, and he was probably laughing secretly at her. No, she couldn't face him now, not to save her own life!

But there was no possibility of avoiding him. Sighing miserably, she crawled out of bed. She was refreshed by a hot bath that soothed her aches and pains. After much deliberation, she decided to wear a dress of shimmering olive-green faille that brightened her eyes to emerald. The maid came to assist her with the tightening of her corset laces, and spent a long time fastening the tiny loops and buttons on the back of her dress. The skirt was pulled tightly over her figure in front and gathered behind in a modest bustle topped by a huge bow. Painstakingly Laura twisted and re-twisted her hair into a perfect coiled chignon and anchored the chestnut mass with a gold comb.

Finally there was nothing left to do. She squared her shoulders and walked downstairs. She was relieved to discover that the men had not yet returned. Some women were attending to their needlework in the parlor, while others lingered in the breakfast room. The food was being kept in crested silver warming dishes, and Laura inspected the array with a smile.

Sophia knew how to serve the proper Bostonian breakfast, the heavy old-fashioned kind. The sideboards fairly groaned under the weight of fruit, oatmeal, preserves and molasses, waffles, biscuits, toasted bread, eggs, cheese, and custard. There was a variety of meats, including chicken with cream gravy, ham, and smoked fish. An empty plate held a few crumbs of what had once been an apple pie. As far as New Englanders were concerned, there was never an inappropriate time of day to serve apple pie.

"Everything will be cleared away soon,"

Sophia told her. "Come, have something to eat."

A plate was thrust in her hands, and Laura smiled, picking up a tidbit here and there. But she was too nervous to eat, and in spite of her sister's entreaties, she barely touched the food.

"More tea?" Sophia asked, hovering about her with maternal concern. "Chocolate?"

"No, thank you," Laura replied absently. She stood up. "I think I'll find something to read. Or perhaps I'll try my hand at the piano again. I have missed playing—I'd forgotten how soothing it is. I'll close the door so as not to disturb anyone."

"Yes, do whatever you like," Sophia said, regarding her with a touch of worry. "Laura, you don't seem quite yourself this morning."

"Don't I?" She felt her cheeks turn pink. "I'm perfectly well."

Sophia lowered her voice to a whisper. "Just set my fears to rest and I'll ask nothing else: Jason treated you kindly, didn't he?"

"Yes, he was kind," Laura whispered back. She leaned closer as if to impart a highly personal secret, and Sophia tilted her head obligingly. "I am going to the piano now."

Smiling wryly, Sophia waved her away.

Laura seated herself at the small rosewood piano with a sigh, her fingers running over the ivory keys as if waiting for inspiration to strike. Then they settled in a pattern she remembered from long ago, a melody that was melancholy and sweet. It suited her mood perfectly. She fumbled a few times, her touch uncertain from lack of practice. As she played, concentrating on the music, she sensed the parlor door opening. Her fingers slowed, then stilled. All she could hear was carpet-muffled footsteps, but she knew who the intruder was.

A pair of strong hands slid over her shoulders, up the sides of her neck, back down. The palms were warm, the fingertips cool. A low, vibrant voice sent a thrill down her spine. "Don't stop."

She pulled her hands from the keys and turned to face Jason as he sat on the small bench beside her. He had never looked so fresh and vital, his hair attractively tousled and his skin ruddy from the icy breezes outside.

For a moment they stared at each other, measuring, asking silent questions. Laura dropped her gaze, and it happened to fall on the muscled thigh pressed close to her own. She remembered that thigh wedged between hers, and embarrassment rushed over her.

"You left me this morning," she heard herself say.

Jason leaned over her downbent head, unable to resist nuzzling the nape of her neck. "I didn't want to wake you. You were sleeping so deeply."

She shivered at the heat of his breath and tried to stand up, only to have him catch her firmly around the waist and pull her back down. Automatically she braced her arms against his chest. "Look at me," he said quietly, "and tell me why you're skittish today."

Laura's fingers plucked nervously at his black-and-tan brocaded vest. "You know why."

"Yes, I know why."

She heard the trace of amusement in his tone. Her eyes flew to his, and she saw that the midnight depths were warm with laughter. Immediately she was horror-stricken. Oh, he was laughing at her, he was jeering at the way she had behaved last night, his chaste wife who had moaned and clung to him so wantonly.

"Let go of me," she said, pushing at him in earnest. "I know what you think, and I won't—"

"Do you?" His arms tightened until she was pinned against his chest, and he smiled at her small scarlet face. "I think you're adorable." He dropped a kiss on her forehead while she struggled helplessly. "I think you need to be reminded of a few things." His mouth joined hers, pressing her lips apart. She could not keep from responding any more than she could stop her heart from beating. As her lips clung to his, he let her hands slip free, and her arms wrapped around his neck. Their tongues touched, circled, slid together languorously.

Gradually Jason released her mouth, and she gave a protesting moan. "I think," he said huskily, "you need to be taken back to bed."

Laura's eyes widened with alarm. "You would not embarrass me in front of the others that way."

He kissed her hungrily. "They'll understand."

"They will not! They're Bostonians."

"I think I'll carry you upstairs. Right now."

He made a move as if to lift her, and she clutched at his shoulders.

"Jason, no, you can't . . ." Her voice trailed off as she saw that he was only teasing her. Her frown of worry dissolved into a scowl.

"Laura," he murmured with a smile, "do you need proof of how much I want you?" He drew her hand to his loins, and she caught her breath at the feel of him, hard and urgent, more than ready to take her. "I never thought it was possible to want a woman so much," he said against her ear. "And if it weren't for your blessed modesty, I *would* take you upstairs . . . or right here . . . anywhere . . ." He sought her lips, his mouth soft and coaxing, setting fire to every nerve.

"Jason," she whispered, leaning against him, "you would tell me if I displeased you last night, wouldn't you?"

"*Displeased* me . . ." he repeated in astonishment. "Laura, no one has ever pleased me *more*. Where did you come by such an idiotic notion?" Suddenly his dark eyes were stern. "If that's what you're fretting about, we really are going upstairs."

This time he was clearly *not* teasing. Alarmed, Laura tried to appease him. "No, I believe you, Jason, I do—"

"Convince me," he challenged, and choked off her words with a sultry kiss. She twisted to fit him more closely, her fingers sliding between his vest and shirt. The pounding of his heart was as wild as her own. She was lost in a wave of sweet madness, not caring what happened next, dimly aware that she would not object if Jason pulled her to the floor and took her right there.

They were interrupted by the harsh clanging of a tin drum and a shrill, metallic blast. The sounds seemed to pierce Laura's eardrums and sent a shock through her body. Jason let go of her with a muffled curse and nearly fell off the piano bench. Together they stared at the intruders.

A pair of giggling imps stood before them. It was Sophia's children, Wilfred and Millicent, holding tin instruments and banging them loudly.

"Lovely children," Jason remarked pleasantly, reaching up to rub the back of his neck, where every hair was standing up straight.

"You were kissing Aunt Laura!" Millicent cried in glee.

"So I was," Jason agreed.

Wilfred pushed up his glasses and squinted at them. "Uncle Hale said to come play for you."

Jason looked at Laura with a rueful grin. "Excuse me. I have two little elves to catch."

"What will you do when you catch them?" she asked in pretend worry.

He smiled darkly. "Bury them outside in the nearest snowdrift."

Wilfred and Millicent screamed in delighted terror and scampered from the room as Jason chased them.

"Don't forget Hale," Laura called after him, and laughed.

In the days that followed Laura was unable to let go of the feeling that she was in a delightful dream that would end with cruel suddenness. Each morning she awakened with a sense of worry that dissolved only when she saw Jason's smile. It was miraculous to her that the husband she had come to dread was now the person she wanted to be with every minute.

Now that she was no longer afraid of his biting

sarcasm being turned on her, she talked freely with him. He was an entertaining companion, sometimes thoughtful and quiet, sometimes roughly playful. He was a considerate lover, always sensitive to her pleasure, but with an earthiness that she found exciting.

To Laura's surprise, Jason seemed to relish the discovery that she was not the delicate, reserved creature he had thought her. One morning he swept her away from the others and took her on a ramble through the woods, teasing and flirting as if she were a maiden he was bent on seducing. Saucily she ducked away when he would have kissed her.

"No," she said, picking up her skirts and making her way to a fallen tree trunk. "I know what you intend, and I will not be taken advantage of in the snow."

He followed readily. "I could make you forget the cold."

"I don't think so." Primly she stepped over the tree trunk, and gave a little shriek as he made a grab for her.

"I never back down from a challenge," he said.

Swiftly she picked up a long birch stick and

turned to face him, touching it to his chest as if it were a sword. "So this is the reason you brought me out here," she accused, "for an unseemly frolic in the middle of the woods."

"Exactly." With deliberate slowness he took the stick and broke it in half, tossing it aside. "And I'm going to have my way with you."

Backing up step by step, Laura considered the possibility of compromise. "One kiss," she offered.

He continued to stalk her. "You'll have to do better than that."

Her eyes sparkled with laughter, and she held out her arms to keep him at bay. "I will not bargain with you, Jason."

They eyed each other assessingly, each waiting for the other to make the first move. Suddenly Laura darted to the side, and found herself snatched up in a pair of strong arms. She laughed exuberantly while he lifted her by the waist as if she weighed nothing at all. Slowly he let her slide down until their faces were even, her feet still dangling above the ground. Without thinking, she twined her arms around his neck and fastened her mouth to his in a kiss so direct and natural that Jason staggered slightly, his senses electrified. He had to put her down before he sent them both tumbling in a heap. Spellbound, he stared at the woman in his arms and thought of what an arrogant fool he'd been. He'd assumed he knew her so well when he didn't know her at all.

"Jason," she asked wistfully, "do we really have to go back home tomorrow?"

"We can't stay here forever."

She sighed and nodded, wondering how long the truce between them would last once they were back in all-too-familiar territory.

It was with reluctance that they finally left the Marshes' Brookline home the next day and returned to their own Beacon Street address. Sophia had been able to guess at Laura's remaining worries and gave Laura an uncharacteristically long hug good-bye. "Everything will be all right," Sophia whispered, patting her on the back. "After seeing Jason with you the past few days, I've come to realize that there is no difficulty of yours that time will not solve."

Laura smiled and nodded, but she knew that in this matter Sophia wasn't right. Time meant very little. Two whole months of marriage had not accomplished for her and Jason what the past four days had. And there were problems that still faced them, problems that could not be resolved no matter how much time went by. She had to find some way of prying past Jason's deepest reserve, the barrier that kept them from reaching an intimacy beyond the physical pleasure they shared.

As he had promised, Jason took her to the site of his most recent building. It was the first time she had actually seen one of his projects under construction. Before now she been wary of showing too much interest in his business concerns. Now she inundated him with questions.

"What sort of people will be renting the apartments?" she asked. "Small families? Young men?"

"And young women, on a cooperative basis."

"Young women without chaperones?"

He laughed at her faintly censorious tone. "Yes, self-reliant women with their own careers, sharing an apartment together. Is that too radical a proposition for a Prescott to approve of?"

"Yes," she said. "But I suppose the Prescotts cannot hold back progress."

He grinned and drew her arm tighter through his. "We'll make a liberal of you yet."

As Jason walked her around the property, Laura was impressed, even a little awed, by the size of the undertaking. The air was thick with the noise of the steam shovel, the crew of men spreading gravel and swearing, the dust everywhere. Part of the property included a former rubbish dump, which was being covered with clean gravel.

The slight train of Laura's skirt dragged through the patches of muddy ground, and she paused every now and then to tug at it impatiently. She was outfitted in the most practical garments she owned, a wool and grosgrain walking dress of a deep plum color, a matching cape, and sealskin boots with double soles. The heavy draperies and tightly molded skirt prevented her from moving with Jason's ease, and he was forced to cut his strides to match hers.

Jason slowed their pace even more as they were approached by a thin, ragged figure from the street. Laura's eyes darkened with pity as she looked at the elderly man, who wore tattered clothes that were hardly adequate protection against the cold. His gray beard was thin and yellowed, his skin veined, and he reeked of gin. He spoke in a heavy Irish brogue that Laura could barely decipher.

"Here now, sir, d'ye have a coin t' spare for an ould man? The wind is sthrong an' could today."

Laura looked up at Jason, whose expression was unreadable. "Indeed it is," he said. He reached into his pocket and pulled out some coins, placing them in the outstretched hand.

The old man peered at him with watery eyes that suddenly brightened with interest. "Sure now, yer frae the ould sod."

Jason's slight accent became more pronounced than usual. "My grandfather left County Wexford during the first potato rot."

"Aye, ye have th' look o' Wexford, eyes an' hair black as coal. Meself, I come frae Cork." The man nodded in thanks, gesturing with the coins clutched tight in his bony fist. "God bless ye, sir, an' yer bonny wife."

Laura glanced back at him as they moved on;

he was scurrying furtively across the street, hands tucked underneath his arms. "Poor man," she said. "I hope he buys something to eat."

"He'll spend it on drink," Jason said flatly.

"How can you be certain?"

For a moment she thought he wasn't going to reply. "He can get whiskey cheaper than bread," he finally said.

"Then why did you give the money to him if you knew . . ." Laura frowned and stared at the ground, feeling the tension in his arm, knowing that something had struck a raw nerve.

Jason felt a powerful urge to tell her what he was thinking, but his habit of privacy concerning his past warned him against saying anything. He opened and closed his mouth several times, feeling heat creep up from his collar as he fought an inner battle. There was no reason to confess anything to her, no need for her to know. And if Laura understood what his childhood had really been like, she would feel contempt for him. She would feel the same disgust that he felt whenever he remembered it. God knew why now of all times he felt driven to tell her what he had once vowed never to speak of.

Jason stopped walking and turned his gaze

to the steam shovel as it bit into the hard ground.

"What is it?" she asked gently. "What did he remind you of?"

He spoke as if the words were being dragged out of him. "I knew men like that when I was young. Men driven from their home by poverty and disease, and most of all hunger. They didn't care where they went, so long as they escaped from Ireland. Often they landed in Boston with no money, no work, no relatives. They . . ." He stopped and took a short breath before continuing. "They used to beg for a warm place in my family's room at night, when the winter was bitter."

"Your family's room? Don't you mean your house?"

He didn't look at her. "We lived in one room of a basement. No plumbing or windows. No light except when the door to the sidewalk above was opened. Filth kept draining in from the street. It was little more than a gutter."

Laura was silent with amazement. That could not be true, she thought. He could not have come from that kind of poverty. She had known the Morans had not been a family of great means, but Jason was talking as if they had been slum-dwellers!

"But your father was a grocer, wasn't he?" she asked awkwardly. "He had enough money to send you to school."

"That was later, when his business began to succeed. Even then he had to trade his soul for the money. He managed to convince some local merchants and politicians that I would be a worthwhile investment." Jason's mouth twisted. "For the first several years my father ran his grocery in our cellar room. Until I was nine or ten, I remember eating nothing but scraps and foodstuffs gone bad, the worst of whatever he couldn't sell."

"But your education . . . How . . . ?"

"My father was one of the few who allowed—no, pushed—his sons into the free public schools. He couldn't read. He wanted at least one of us to be able to."

"Did you want to?"

"At first I didn't care. I was an uneducated brute who wanted nothing except food and what little comfort I could find. And there is an attitude in the North End, that a man isn't meant to rise above the life he's born to. The

Irish are fatalistic about such things. I thought the only way to get something I wanted was to steal it." Jason smiled grimly. "When I couldn't find coal or wood to scavenge, the family had to stay in bed all day to keep warm. God knows I saw no use in learning to read."

"What made you decide to try?"

He answered distantly, as if he were only half-aware of her presence. The memories were never far from his mind—they were what drove him—but until now he had never allowed himself to speak of them. "I saw men laboring on the wharves until their backs were ruined. And the hostlers and stablers living in worse conditions than the horses they cared for. All the Irish laborers and domestics who will work for any wage—they call them 'green hands.' There was nothing I wouldn't have done to escape it." Jason looked at her then, his black eyes unnervingly intense. "I worked all the time. On the docks, in saloons, anywhere there was a coin to be made. In school I studied hard, made the highest marks. I never lost at anything— baseball, footraces, public debates. Every man of means I crossed paths with became a mentor. But the admission into the Boston Latin

School was nothing short of a miracle. I'll owe favors for that from now until kingdom come. That was when everything changed, when I finally knew what it was I really wanted."

Laura did not ask what that was, for she was afraid of the answer. She suspected that what Jason really wanted was what he could never have, to assume a place in the most powerful circles of Boston society that would never be allowed to an Irishman. Such positions had been decided generations ago, and no intruders were admitted into the sacred circles. No matter how much money or power Jason acquired, he would always be considered an outsider.

"And then Boston Latin led to college," she prompted quietly.

"When it came time for that, some Irish businessmen helped to foot the bill. I eventually repaid their investments many times over."

"Your family must be very proud of you," she said, and was puzzled when he didn't answer.

While she was still trying to absorb all of what he had told her, Jason took her by the shoulders, his gaze hunting for pity or revulsion. She felt neither, only a desire to comfort him. She thought of what he must have been like as a boy, hungry and too poor to hope or even to dream.

"Oh, Jason," she said softly. "I didn't suspect you had such desperate odds against you. You should have told me before."

She saw that whatever he had been expecting from her, it had not been that. His face was utterly still. She touched his lean cheek with her gloved hand.

"You should be repelled, knowing where I came from," he muttered.

Laura shook her head. "I admire you for it. I admire you for what you've made of yourself."

He gave no reply, staring at her in an almost calculating way, as if he wanted to believe her but could not. Her hand fell to her side, and she gave him an uncertain smile.

They were interrupted by the approach of the construction foreman, who had seen them from a distance. Eagerly he greeted them and conferred with Jason on some details of the project. Laura watched them, struck by how quickly the bitterness and memories on Jason's face had vanished, replaced by his usual calm authority. It dismayed her to see how easily he hid his feelings. She was afraid she would never fully understand him.

After bidding the foreman good-bye, they walked to the double barouche and Jason muttered to the driver that they were going home. Laura clambered into the velvet-lined carriage, arranging the mass of her bustle, petticoats, and heavily draped skirts in order to sit comfortably. Jason sat beside her, closed the door, and pulled the morocco blinds at the window shut. Obligingly he leaned over to help tug a fold of her skirt out from beneath her. The carriage started with a small jolt.

"Jason," she said in a low voice.

"Yes?"

"I hope you don't regret telling me about your past." Hesitantly she reached out to stroke his chest. "I know there is much more you've left unsaid. Someday I hope you will trust me enough to tell me the rest."

His hand closed in a fist over hers. Surprised, she darted a look at him, wondering if she had somehow made him angry. There was a dark blaze in his eyes—but it was not anger. He wrapped his other hand around the back of her neck. His thick black lashes lowered, and he looked at her with a narrowed gaze.

"Laura, why did you marry me?" he asked roughly.

She was startled, and turned a shade or two paler. Clumsily she tried to dodge the question by making light of it. "I believe this is called fishing for a compliment, Mr. Moran." She smiled, but he did not respond. His silence forced her to continue. "Why did I want to marry you . . . well, there were many reasons, I suppose. I . . . I knew you would be a good provider, and you were Hale's friend, and during those four years you spent Christmas with us, I became acquainted with you, and . . ." Her gaze dropped away. She tried to pry herself free, but she was held fast against one hundred and eighty pounds of obstinate male, and they both knew she would not be freed until she gave him what he wanted.

"The truth," he muttered.

"I can't tell you something I don't know."

"Try."

Helplessly she tugged at her trapped hand. "Why is it necessary?"

"Because I thought I'd forced you into marrying me. A few days ago you told me that you married me of your own free will. I have to know why."

"I don't *know* why." Laura gasped as he twisted and dragged her across his lap. She was bound in a cocoon of skirts and stays, her head forced up by the pressure of his arm. "Jason, please, I don't know what you want—"

"The hell you don't."

"Let me go, you bully!"

He ignored her demand. "Then we'll take another tack. If you had a choice, then tell me why you didn't marry someone from your own social rank. There were young men with good names and adequate means—you could have had any of them."

"Oh, a prime selection," she agreed, glaring at him. "Hordes of blue-blooded snobs reared to do nothing except preserve the money their grandfathers made. I could have married some dignified Brahmin who would insist on eating oatmeal every morning of his life, and tucking an umbrella under his arm even when it wasn't raining, and complaining until he was an old man about not being accepted into the Porcellian club at Harvard!"

"Why didn't you?"

"Jason, stop this!" She writhed until her strength was exhausted.

"You told me you wanted to marry me since you were fifteen," he said ruthlessly. "Why?"

She trembled with distress, her eyes glittering with sudden tears.

"No, don't cry," he said, his voice gentling. "Laura, I've told you things I've never confessed to anyone. It can't be any more difficult for you than it was for me."

His handsome face was so close to hers, and there was something pagan in the blackness of his eyes. Laura drew the tip of her tongue over her dry lips and swallowed. Her blood was rushing so fast it made her light-headed. "The first time I met you," she managed to say, "Hale had brought you home for the Christmas holidays. You kept watching me during that awful dinner . . . remember?"

He nodded slightly.

"You looked like a wolf in a cage," she said. "The room seemed too small for you. You didn't belong there, but I could see how badly you wanted to, how determined you were. And I knew I could help you."

"Dammit, you didn't marry me to be helpful!"

Futilely she tried to free her arms. "We'll be arriving home soon—"

"I won't let you go until I have the answer. Was it that you liked the idea of marrying a social inferior? So you could always have the whip hand?"

"No," she gasped.

"The money? You wanted to be the wife of a rich man, no matter how vulgar his bloodlines."

"Jason, you . . . you louse!" She struggled furiously. Had she been able to slap his face, she would have.

"Why did you marry me?"

"Because I was a fool, and I thought you needed me, and I—" She was so upset she was shaking, and she was terrified to realize she was on the verge of blurting out the truth.

"Why did you marry me?" came the relentless demand.

Her eyes stung sharply. "Jason, don't make me—"

"*Why?*"

"Because I love you," she choked, finally goaded into defeat. "I've loved you from the first moment I saw you. That was the only reason . . . the only one."

Four

$\mathcal{A}$ tremor went through Jason's body, and he pressed his lips to her forehead. He had never wanted anyone to love him before. There had never been room in his life for anything or anyone who would distract him from his ambition. Until his engagement, there had been affairs, but never without the mutual understanding that they were temporary. Laura was the only woman he had wanted for always.

"You're cruel," she sobbed, wondering what she had just done. It had been the mistake of her life to admit her feelings so soon. She should have waited, should have held her ground. "You're a bully, and selfish, and—"

"Yes, and a louse," he murmured, brushing her tears away. He kissed her wet eyelids. "Don't cry, *mo stoir*, don't."

Desperate to soothe her, he kissed her with all the gentleness he was capable of. He reached down and pulled her arms around his neck, while his tongue flickered in her mouth. His muscled arm was hard against her back. Slowly her tears ceased, and her trembling fingers slid into his hair.

At this sign of her response, Jason finished the kiss with an infinitely soft stroke of his tongue and took his mouth from hers. He had to stop now, or he wouldn't be able to control himself. But her slim body molded to his, and her breasts shifted against his chest. He tried to move her off his lap. "We'll be home soon," he said gruffly, more to himself than to her. "We'll be home and then—"

Her red lips pressed against his, sweetly luring him away from sanity. Greedily Jason angled his mouth over hers, his tongue thrusting savagely. She writhed in response to the painful throb between her legs and returned his passion with equal force. His hand searched frantically through the mass of her skirts for her legs, her thighs, unable to reach any part of her through the tightly binding garments.

The carriage stopped, and Jason tensed with a muffled curse. Laura gasped incoherently, her fingers clenching into his coat. It took several seconds for her to understand that they were home. She looked at Jason, her gaze unfocused. Her hair was falling around her shoulders, pins dropping right and left, her hat dislodged, and her clothes disheveled.

Clumsily she raised her hands to her hair, flushing with mortification. She thought of the way the maids would giggle at the story of the cool, composed Mrs. Moran walking in with her clothes askew and her hair looking like a bird's nest.

The driver began to open the carriage door from the outside, and Jason caught at it easily. With a brief word to the driver, he pulled the door shut. Turning to Laura, he watched her twist handfuls of hair and jab pins in her chignon. "Can I help?"

"You have helped quite enough," she said in agitation. "How like you this is! When you want something you must have it regardless of time or place, and all other considerations be damned."

"When it comes to you," he said, "yes."

She glanced at him then, and found a caressing warmth in his eyes that caused her hands to falter. Painstakingly she rearranged her clothes, repositioned her hat, and gave him a nod when she was ready to leave the carriage.

After he walked her up the steps and into the entrance hall, Laura stopped in the middle of the polished parquet floor. Quickly the housekeeper came to take her cape and Jason's coat. "Mrs. Ramsey," Laura murmured to the housekeeper, "I'll be down soon to discuss the plans for dinner. First I must change from my walking dress."

"Yes, Mrs. Moran. I shall send one of the maids to help you—"

"That won't be necessary," Jason interrupted matter-of-factly, taking Laura's elbow.

The housekeeper's face wore a mixture of speculation and delighted horror. Clearly she wondered what might take place upstairs. It was still broad daylight outside—an unthinkable time for a husband to lay with his wife.

"Yes, sir," she said, and headed for the kitchen.

Laura tried to pull her elbow from his. "Jason, I don't know what you intend, but—"

"Don't you?" He guided her up the stairs without the slightest appearance of hurry.

"This can wait until evening," she whispered. "I know you must have many things to attend to—"

"Yes, important things."

As soon as they reached her room, he yanked her inside and closed the door with his foot. His mouth covered hers impatiently, his breath a scalding rush against her cheek. He pulled off her hat and worked at her hair, scattering pins until the long chestnut locks fell down to her waist.

"Jason, I need time to think about all that has happened—"

"You can think about everything to your heart's desire. Later." His hands moved restlessly from her breasts to her hips. "Did you mean what you said in the carriage?"

"About your being a bully?" She tilted her head back as his lips found the sensitive hollow beneath her ear. "Yes, I meant every word."

"About loving me."

It would be useless to deny it now. Laura swallowed and forced herself to meet his dark eyes. Jason looked almost stern, his mouth set with a firmness that made her want to cover it with enticing kisses. "Yes," she said huskily, "I meant that too."

Without another word he turned her around and unfastened the back of her dress. In his haste, his fingers were less agile than usual. The heavy dress collapsed along with masses of petticoats. Laura heaved a sigh of relief as her corset laces were untied and the contraption of stays and silk was tossed to the other side of the room. She heard the sound of cloth ripping and felt her torn cambric drawers slip to the floor.

Shivering, she leaned back against him, her head dropping on his shoulder. His palm rubbed in a circle over her abdomen. "Tell me again," he said against the perfumed softness of her neck.

"I love you . . . Jason . . ."

He turned her in his arms and hungrily sought her mouth with his, while he pulled the hem of her chemise up to her waist. Laura responded lovingly, her lips parting, her body arching to his. But as she felt the demanding pressure of his arousal against the inside of her thigh, she pulled away from him.

"No, we can't," she said. "I must get dressed and go downstairs. Mrs. Ramsey will be waiting—"

"Mrs. Ramsey be damned. Take off the chemise."

"I shouldn't," she said weakly.

"Don't you want to?" He approached her slowly, and she backed away until her shoulders bumped against the wall. She was mesmerized by the darkness of his eyes. When he stared at her like that, she could refuse him nothing. Unsteadily she grasped the hem of the chemise and pulled it over her head.

Jason reached for her, his hands sliding over her back and buttocks. She wrapped her arms around his neck, every nerve kindling with the intense passion he aroused. Murmuring to her hoarsely, he lifted her against the wall, the muscles in his arms bulging. Her eyes widened, and she gasped in surprise as she felt him enter her in a hard, deep thrust. Obeying his whispered commands, she wrapped her silk-stockinged legs around his hips.

"You're so beautiful," he rasped, kissing her

chin, her cheeks, her parted lips. "So sweet . . . Laura . . ."

Rhythmically he withdrew and thrust into her warm body, staring at her flushed face. Laura whimpered and tightened her legs, her heels digging into his muscled buttocks. She clung to him, her hands grasping frantically at his sweat-slick shoulders. Suddenly the exquisite tension coiled inside, tightening painfully. Gasping, she buried her face against his neck and felt herself burning slowly, slowly, her body consumed in a blaze of pleasure. Jason gritted his teeth as he strove to prolong the moment, but he was soon overtaken by his own release.

After a long time, Laura became aware that her toes were touching the floor. She was wrapped tightly in his arms. Hazily she thought that she had never felt so safe, so protected. She pressed her lips to his shoulder. "I've always loved you," she whispered, stroking the dark hair at the nape of his neck. "Even when you were cruel to me, even when you looked at me as though you hated me."

"I wanted to hate you."

"And did you?"

"Almost," he admitted gruffly. "When I saw you with Perry Whitton. I couldn't stand the sight of another man's hands on you." He smiled ruefully. "I'd never felt jealousy before, and suddenly it was twisting at my guts. I wanted to strangle you only a little less than I did Whitton."

"There was no need to be jealous," she murmured, still stroking his hair. "I've never wanted anyone but you."

Laura hummed carols as she hung gilded eggshells on the Christmas tree, which was small enough that she could reach all but the top branches. It was a week before Christmas, and she had been busy for days with holiday baking and decorating the house. The scent of evergreens filled the parlor, bringing to mind many childhood memories. Since she had not had time to make more than a few simple ornaments, her mother and Sophia had each given her a few to begin her own collection, including the angel with glass wings that she had loved since childhood. Painstakingly she and one of the maids had strung cranberries to fill the empty spaces, and their fingers were reddened and sore after hours of work. The rest of the room was decorated with garlands of holly, wreaths of gilded lemon leaves, pinecone clusters, and gold velvet ribbons.

Idly Laura wondered how Jason's family would spend Christmas. They would probably gather relatives and friends at their home, sharing memories, talking and feasting together. Laura wished that she dared ask Jason about the Morans, and why they had not sent any invitations or cards. She had only seen a few of her in-laws once. Since Jason's father, Charles, had passed away a few years before, his mother Kate had attended the wedding with some of her children, two of her daughters and one of her young sons. They had not come to the reception afterward. The Morans had been nicely, if plainly dressed, and they'd seemed to be quietly awed by their surroundings. "Brogues you could have cut with a knife," her mother had said disdainfully.

In the past year Laura had exchanged short letters with Jason's mother Kate, but that was the limit of their interaction. She knew from those notes that Jason visited his family infrequently, always during his workday. He never invited Laura or mentioned the visits to her afterward—it was as if his family didn't exist, as if she and they occupied separate worlds that only Jason could traverse.

Deep in thought, Laura tapped her forefinger against her lips. She wished she could pay Kate Moran a visit. There were many questions about Jason that Kate could answer if she cared to. Laura wanted to know more about her husband, more about the past he found so difficult to talk about. Of course, if she asked for Jason's permission to visit the Morans, he would not allow it. And if she went without his knowledge, there was the chance that he would find out.

"I don't care," she muttered. "I have every right to see them." She squared her small jaw. "I *will* see them." Filled with a mixture of determination and guilt—for she disliked the idea of doing something behind Jason's back—she considered the best time to do it. Tomorrow morning, she decided, after Jason left for work.

The Moran home was located in a solidly middle-class section of Charlestown. The two- and three-family houses had once been inhabited by the well-to-do but were now occupied by the overflow of immigrants from the adjoining neighborhood. The street was well-kept, completely unlike the strings of crowded flats and garbage-filled passageways of the South End slum districts.

Laura emerged from the carriage and looked up and down the cobblestone street with interest. It was a dry, brisk day. Lines of work clothes, colored blue, gray, and brown, flapped in the breeze. The air was filled with the scent of stewing meat and vegetables. A young couple walked by her, their arms linked, their heads swathed in knitted caps and scarves. They threw her a few discreet glances but did not slow their pace. A few children interrupted their game of stickball to stand and stare at her and the elegant carriage.

After telling the driver to wait in front of the house, Laura went to the door unescorted. There was no brass knocker. She hesitated, then lifted her hand to rap on the scarred paneled wood.

A boy's voice came from behind her. "Yer knockin' at *my* house!"

Laura turned and was confronted by a small boy of eight or nine. A smile crossed her lips. He was a Moran, no question of it. He had black hair and dark eyes, fair skin, and ruddy cheeks that had not yet lost their childish roundness. His belligerent chin and aggressive nose pointed up at her.

"Donal?" she guessed, knowing that was the name of one of Jason's two brothers.

"Robbie," the boy corrected indignantly. "An who might ye be?"

"I'm Laura Moran." When that elicited no sign of recognition, she added, "Your brother Jason's wife."

"Ooohhh." Robbie regarded her wisely. "Ma says yer a foine lady. What d'ye want?"

"I would like to see your mother."

He grasped the door handle in both hands, tugged it open, and held it for her. "Ma!" he barked into the house, and gestured for Laura to go inside. "Ma, 'tis Jason's wife!"

He urged Laura to accompany him down a long, narrow hallway lined with garments hanging on hooks. The hall led to the kitchen, where she could see the side of the cast-iron stove. There was a graniteware pot on top of the stove, and the air smelled of stewing apples. "Er . . . Robbie, perhaps I should not come in unannounced," she said.

He was puzzled by the strange word. "Unan . . ."

"Perhaps you should tell your mother that I'm here."

"Sure now, I'm tellin' 'er," he interrupted, and called shrilly toward the kitchen. "Ma, 'tis Jason's wife!"

"Who is it, ye say?" came a woman's voice, and Robbie took hold of Laura's arm, triumphantly dragging her past the stove to the wooden table in the center of the kitchen.

Kate Moran, a sturdy, pleasant-faced woman in her mid forties, regarded Laura with round blue eyes. A wooden rolling pin dropped from her hands onto the piecrust in front of her. "God save us," she exclaimed. "Jason's wife!"

"I apologize for the unexpected intrusion," Laura began, but her voice was lost in the bustle that suddenly filled the room. Jason's sisters, both attractive girls in their teens, rushed in to see the visitor.

" 'Tis Jason?" Kate asked anxiously, her flour-coated hands pressed to her heavy bosom. "Och, somethin' has happened to me firstbarn, me precious boy—"

"No, no," Laura said, "Jason is fine. Perfectly

302

fine. I've just come for . . ." She paused, conscious of the many curious gazes on her. "I've just come for a visit," she said lamely. "But I can see that you're busy. Perhaps some other time would be better?"

There was a moment of stillness. Kate recovered quickly, her worry replaced by curiosity. " 'Tis plaised we are that ye are here. P'raps a cup o' tea—Maggie, fetch the teapot, an' Polly, show the lady to the parlor—"

"I wouldn't mind staying in the kitchen," Laura ventured. She was conscious of the family's dumbfounded gazes as she eased herself into one of the wooden chairs at the table. The room was warm and cheerful, and she preferred its informal atmosphere.

Kate shrugged helplessly. " 'Tis here ye'll stay, then." She shooed the children from the room and gave Laura a measuring glance. "An' now tell me what yer about, me dear. To be sure, Jason knows nothin' of yer visit."

"No, he does not," Laura admitted, unconsciously resting her elbows on the flour-dusted oilcloth that covered the table. She hesitated before adding, "I've come to talk to you in the hopes that you would be able to explain some things about his past to me. Jason isn't an easy man to understand."

Kate gave a short laugh. "Nay, there's no understandin' that contrary, prideful boy, nor his fine notions. A hard head like his pa's."

Laura was barely aware of time passing as she sat in the kitchen with Jason's mother. The tea grew cold in their cups while the conversation lengthened. Kate's mood relaxed from careful politeness to amiability. It was clear that she liked to talk, and in Laura she found an encouraging listener. She brought out an old photograph of Charlie Moran so that Laura could see the resemblance between father and son. " 'Twas tuck the first day Charlie opened the store on Causeway," Kate said, beaming with pride.

"He was very handsome," Laura replied, struck by the similarity to her husband—except that Charlie Moran's face had been weathered and harshly lined by years of poverty and backbreaking labor. There was the hint of a smile in his eyes, however, and a vulnerable quality that was very different from Jason's dark, cynical gaze.

"I nivver showed this to Jason," Kate commented.

"Why not? I think he would like to see it."

"Nay, not after the way they left off."

"There was a falling-out?"

Kate nodded vigorously. "It started wi' that fancy school, that taught him that uppish talk an' them high-tone words. Och, the boys tuck it on themselves to tease. An' his pa told him not to spake so high-an-mighty."

Laura thought of how isolated Jason must have been, caught between two worlds. "But his father must have been proud of him," she said. "It was remarkable for an Irish boy to attend Boston Latin, and then college—"

"Aye, Charlie near to burst his buttons." Kate paused. "But he fretted over it too, he did."

"Why?"

"Charlie said 'twas too much schoolin' by far. An' he was right, it tuck me Jason away fer good."

"Took him away?"

"Aye, 'twas plain as day. Jason would have none o' the girls in the neighborhood, foine girls though they were. He would have none o' his father's store, an' none o' his family. The local lads pressed him to take a position at the *Pilot*—'tis an Irish paper, dear. He could've gathered a followin' that would've led him to the state legislature. But Jason said he wanted nothin' but to mind his own affairs." Kate shook her head. "Ashamed he was to be Irish, an' to be the son o' Charlie Moran. 'Twas that they argued over the day before me poor Charlie died. Two stubborn divvils."

"He passed away during Jason's first year of school, didn't he?" Laura asked.

Kate nodded. "When Jason made his money, he thought to buy me a grand house an' send his brothers an' sisters to school. I told him I'd not give up me home. Donal looks after the store, an' the girls hope to marry wi' good Irish lads—the rest o' me brood cares not a whit for schoolin'. Cut from a diff'runt cloth, Jason was."

"But he needs his family," Laura said. "He does, although he may not realize how much."

Kate was about to reply when Robbie's high-pitched voice called down the hallway. "Ma! 'Tis Jason!"

Laura froze, staring in surprise at the kitchen doorway as her husband's broad-shouldered form appeared. Her heart thumped unpleasantly as she saw the ominous glint in his eyes. "Jason," she said feebly. She stood up and attempted a placating smile. "How did you know . . . ?"

His voice was cool. "I came home early. Mrs. Ramsey told me where you were."

Kate regarded her son placidly. "We've been havin' a nice visit, yer Laura an' me."

His expression didn't change, but he bent and kissed Kate's forehead. "Hello, Ma."

Laura winced as Jason took hold of her arm in a grip that was just short of being painful. "It's time to go home," he said softly, and she realized with a sinking heart that he was angrier than she had feared he would be.

After allowing her barely enough time to bid the Morans farewell, Jason rode back with her in the carriage. The tense silence between them sawed at Laura's nerves until they were shredded. "I wanted to tell you, Jason," she said hesitantly, "but I knew you wouldn't have allowed me to go."

He laughed shortly. "I hope you found the Morans entertaining."

"I—I didn't go to be entertained."

"I don't care why the hell you went. But it's damn well going to be the last time you set foot in Charlestown."

"For heaven's sake, it does no harm to anyone if I choose to see your family! I don't understand why you're taking on so."

"You don't have to understand, although you could if you cared to look beyond the end of your nose. And wipe that wounded look off your face, or I—" He clamped his teeth together, biting off his next words. His face was dark with fury.

"Why won't you let me have anything to do with your family? Why can't we include them in our lives?"

"Damn you!" he exploded. "My life with you has nothing to do with them! I don't want reminders—by God, I won't have you combing through my past for your own amusement! You don't belong in my family any more than I belong in yours. From now on you'll stay away from them." His lips curled in an ugly sneer. "And if you even think of defying me in this, I'll make you sorry in ways your soft little imagination couldn't begin to conceive."

Laura shrank back from his vicious tone, her green eyes alarmed. "Jason, don't threaten me—"

"Do you understand what I've just told you?"

"Jason, please—"

"Do you understand?"

"Yes," she said, hurt and intimidated. "I'll do as you say."

It was rare that Jason drank to excess, but that evening he closeted himself in the library with his whiskey and stayed until well after Laura had retired to bed. He did not come to her room, and she tossed and turned restlessly, missing his warmth and his large, strong body to snuggle against. The next morning she awoke with dark-circled eyes and a sense of injustice. He was trying to punish her, she thought with annoyance. She would show him that she wasn't in the least affected by his withdrawal.

Sitting across the breakfast table from him, she saw with satisfaction that he was suffering from a fierce headache and his eyes were bloodshot. His temper was foul, but he was quiet, and he seemed to find it difficult to look at her. Slowly she realized that his anger was neither petty nor temporary, and that it had less to do with her than with the pain of old wounds. She thought about bringing up the matter of their argument—no, it might be better to keep her silence.

A few days passed, and it was time for them to attend the large Christmas Eve party that Sophia and Judge Marsh were giving. Laura had never felt less like laughing and pretending to be cheerful, but she was determined not to give her friends and family any reason to think she was having troubles with her husband. It took three hours and the help of both maids to dress and arrange her hair.

Her dress was made of deep rose satin, fitted so tightly to her body that there was not a quarter-inch of room to spare. It was embroidered from the square-cut bodice to the hem with thousands of crimson beads sewn in a flowered pattern. A ruffled satin train was draped from the small of her waist down to the floor, flowing gently out from her body as she walked. The sleeves were tight and banded at the wrists with more beads. Ruby combs glittered in the mass of braids and shining curls gathered at the back of her head.

Jason was waiting for her downstairs, his

face expressionless. He was attired in flawless black and white, looking polished and astonishingly handsome. Something flickered in his eyes as he glanced over her, and when his gaze reached her face, she was aware of the feminine flutter of her senses.

An endless line of carriages blocked the street where the Marsh home blazed with light. Women in velvet mantles and furs were escorted to the entrance by men in greatcoats and tall hats. Groups of carolers strolled from house to house, filling the night with music. Hot rum punch garnished with raisins and fruit slices lent its spicy aroma to the air, as did the pine wreaths and bayberry candles in every room.

Hale besieged them as soon as they entered the house, cheerfully kissing Laura and urging Jason to join him for a drink with some of the friends they had gone to college with. Dutifully Laura greeted her mother, who looked as stiffly displeased as usual. Wilhemina Prescott glanced at her youngest daughter assessingly. "And how is the situation between you and . . . that man?"

"You are referring to my husband, Mother?"

Laura asked, and forced a bright smile to her face. "Splendid."

"I have been informed otherwise. You and he engaged in some kind of quarrel at the party you gave last month."

"It has been resolved, Mother."

Wilhemina frowned. "It is shockingly ill-bred to air one's grievances in public, Laura. I hope you are not taking on the coarse, vulgar habits that his sort of people indulge in—"

"Laura!" Sophia's light voice interrupted. "Dear, you must come and see how the children decorated the tree ... absolutely charming ... excuse us, Mother."

"Thank you," Laura said feelingly, trailing after her sister.

"She's in fine form tonight," Sophia muttered. "Father's not with her. She claims he is indisposed. My guess is they have had a row over his most recent fancy-friend."

Laura stayed at Sophia's side for much of the party, while the crowd grew lively with the dancing, music, and potent punch. Her gaze moved around the sea of familiar faces. She caught a glimpse of her husband as he talked with the people gathered around him. It was not difficult to pick Jason out from the crowd—his dark, vivid looks made everyone around him seem colorless in comparison. His manner was livelier and more intense than the cool crispness of the people around him.

Laura smiled slightly. It didn't matter to her if Jason was ever truly accepted by the Boston elite or not. She was glad of the differences between him and the rest of them, glad of his earthy vitality and even his exasperating pride. Impishly she decided to go to him to find some way of enticing him to a private corner. Surely he wouldn't mind a stolen kiss or two.

She made her way through the entrance hall, artfully sweeping up the folds of her train to keep it from being trampled by wayward feet. Hale and one of his friends walked past her to the front door, holding a third young man up by the shoulders. The man was obviously the worse for drink, and they were taking him outside to sober him up in the cold air. Such situations were always handled with dispatch, before the ladies could be offended by the sight of a gentleman in his cups. "Good evening, Mrs. Moran,"

Hale said wryly, grinning at her. "Step aside for Samuel Pierce Lindon, unfortunate victim of hot rum punch."

"Shall I fetch coffee from the kitchen?" she asked sympathetically.

Hale opened his mouth to answer, but he was interrupted by Samuel, whose head wobbled in Laura's direction. "Moran?" he slurred. "You're the sisshter . . . that one who m-married a m-m-mick."

"Yes, I'm that one," Laura said dryly, knowing that the boy would never have dreamed of saying such a thing were he sober.

Drunkenly Samuel lurched out of Hale's grasp and pinned Laura against the front door. "You're standin' under the mishletoe."

"I'm afraid you are mistaken," Laura muttered, shoving her elbows hard into his midriff. He wound his arms tightly around her and refused to let go.

"Here now!" Hale grunted in annoyance, trying to pry Samuel away. "Let go of my sister, half-wit. Sorry, Laura . . . he's too foxed to know what he's doing—"

"You drather have a gennleman than a *mick* in your bed, wouldn' you?" Samuel asked, his liquor-pungent breath wafting in Laura's face. "I'll show you what you're missing . . . One li'l kiss, thas all . . . you greenhorn wives don' usually mind sharing your fav—"

Suddenly Samuel was lifted and spun around as if by a tornado. Laura fell back against the door, aghast as she saw a brief scuffle between Samuel and her husband. Jason's face was white with rage, his black eyes blazing. Feebly Lindon swung and missed. A woman screamed while others swayed in ladylike faints. Jason drew back his fist and dropped the young man with one hard blow. He would have beaten him to a pulp had Hale not pounced on him and held him from behind. The crowd swarmed into the entrance hall, chattering excitedly.

"Easy, Moran," Hale hissed, struggling to keep hold of Jason. "No need to wipe the floor with him. He didn't hurt Laura—I was here."

Jason went still, struggling to control his temper. He shrugged off Hale's restraining arms and strode to his wife, taking her by the shoulders. He looked over her worriedly. "Laura—"

"Jason, I'm all right," she said shakily. "There was no need to make a scene. He's just a drunken boy. He didn't mean to—"

Her mother's icy voice cut through the hubbub. "How dare you," Wilhemina exclaimed, glaring at Jason. "How dare you turn a society gathering into a dockyard brawl! It may be common among the Irish to behave in such a manner, but it is not the way of decent people!" Her tall, thin body stiffened imperiously. "Your expensive clothes and pretend manners cannot conceal what you are, an ill-bred peasant—"

Laura interrupted, unable to stand any more. "Shut up, Mother."

Wilhemina's jaw dropped in astonishment. None of her children had ever dared to speak to her so rudely.

Hale snickered, throwing Laura a glance of surprised approval.

Sophia stepped forward and shook her finger at Samuel, who had managed to sit up and was holding his head bemusedly. "Young man, I do not appreciate having my guests accosted in my own home." She turned to her brother. "Please take your friend outside, Hale."

"Yes, ma'am," he replied dutifully.

"Sophia," Laura said in a low voice, slipping her arm through Jason's, "I believe we will be going home now."

Sophia looked from Jason's stony expression to Laura's distressed one. "I understand, dear."

Hale stopped them before they reached the door, clapping Jason on the back. "I . . . er, would like to apologize for Lindon. He'll be devilish sorry for all of this when he sobers up." He extended a hand and Jason shook it briefly, both of them exchanging rueful glances.

Laura was silent during the carriage ride home, wanting to let both their tempers settle. She was angry and upset by Jason's behavior. It had not been necessary for him to make such a scene! Samuel had been obnoxious but hardly dangerous. The problem could have been solved with a few brief words, and Jason knew it. He also knew that if two gentlemen ever found it necessary to come to blows, it was never done in the presence of ladies.

As soon as Jason escorted Laura into the house, Mrs. Ramsey appeared to welcome them. Laura waved the housekeeper away, and Mrs. Ramsey promptly disappeared, having read from their faces that all was not well. Jason turned and began to head toward the stairs.

"Jason, wait," Laura said, catching hold of his arm. "We must talk about what happened."

He shook off her hand. "There's nothing to talk about."

"Isn't there? You must admit that you over-reacted."

"I don't call it an overreaction to stop some drunken fool from pawing my wife."

"There was no need to deal with him so harshly. He wasn't aware of what he was doing—"

"The hell he wasn't! Do you think he would have insulted you had you been someone else's wife? A Boston Brahmin's wife?" He sneered at her lack of response. "No. Because he and his peers are accustomed to giving the Irish house-maids a slap and tickle, or visiting the North End shanties for prostitutes, and in their eyes the fact that you're married to an Irishman makes you—"

"Jason, don't," she cried, throwing her arms around his neck and hugging herself to his rigid body. "Must you blame everything on the fact that you're Irish?" She pressed a beseeching kiss on the side of his neck. "Let's talk about this sensibly." She gave him another kiss, this time underneath his ear. "Come sit with me by the fire."

For a moment she thought he was going to

refuse her, but then he agreed with a muffled curse and followed her into the parlor. While Laura drew up an overstuffed ottoman and seated herself, Jason stirred the coals in the grate. He threw on a handful of pine knots and a birch log, dusted off his hands, and sat on the floor, propping one knee up. The blaze of firelight played over his rumpled black hair and hard-edged face, turning his skin to copper.

Laura took a deep breath and groped for the right words to say. "Jason . . . that Lindon boy's remarks didn't upset me as much as your reaction did." She stared into the fire, picking at her beaded dress in agitation. "I'm afraid that you may have more in common with my mother and her prejudices than you think," she said. He gave her a forbidding stare, but she continued doggedly. "Deep down you seem to believe as she does, that a Brahmin should never have married an Irishman. You think the two worlds should be kept separate. But you can never erase your past . . . your family . . . your heritage. You can't turn your back and pretend they don't exist."

Jason was silent, motionless. Laura sighed with frustration, thinking that she may as well have been talking to a brick wall. "Oh, why must you be so stubborn?" After considering him for a moment, she stood up and went to the Christmas tree in the distant corner. "I have something for you," she said, picking up a small package wrapped in colored paper. "I'd rather give it to you now than wait until the morning."

"Laura, I'm not in the mood for this."

"Please," she entreated, bringing the gift to him. "Please, I want you to." Heedless of her fine dress, she knelt on the floor next to him and dropped the flat package into his lap.

He regarded it stonily. "I suppose this has some bearing on the conversation."

"Yes, I think so."

Slowly Jason ripped one side of the paper and pulled out a small photograph in a frame. He went still, his head bent over the sepia-toned albumen print. Laura had chosen a simple silver frame ornamented with a garnet in each corner.

The picture was of Charlie Moran in the doorway of his grocery store. It was a shock to Jason—he had not seen his father's face since the day before Charlie had died. He felt as if he'd received a hard blow to the chest. "Where did you get this?" he asked after a long time.

"Your mother showed it to me. I asked her if

I could give it to you. She said you'd never seen it."

"No." He stared at the weathered face in the photograph, shaken by the memories it provoked.

Laura watched him with an almost maternal tenderness as he studied the faded image.

"Big, hard-drinking, blustering, hot-tempered Irishman," Jason said. "We could never talk without arguing. The last time I saw him was the worst. We nearly came to blows."

"Why?"

"He accused me of being ashamed of him and the family. I told him he was right. I . . ." Jason looked away from the picture, his jaw tensing. ". . . said things I never should have said. I wanted no part of his plans for me. God knows I was never meant to champion Irish causes, or go into ward politics, or take over his store—" He broke off abruptly. "It doesn't matter now."

"He died the next day, didn't he?" Laura asked.

Jason smiled bitterly. "That night, actually. It was quick, unexpected. Ma sent for me, but he was dead before I reached the house."

"You must have been devastated."

"I was angry because of all I'd said to him." Jason was too wrapped up in the memory to guard his words. "Because he'd gone before I could take any of it back."

"What would you have told him?" she whispered.

"I . . ." He swallowed hard and narrowed his eyes against the sudden glitter of tears. "Dammit." Roughly he rubbed his sleeve over his face, disgusted with his lack of control. "Hell, I don't know."

"Jason, you must forgive yourself," she said softly. "There is no one to blame. It wasn't your fault that you wanted a life different from his. It wasn't your fault that he died."

"I never . . ." Jason was surprised at how the memory could hurt after all these years. "I never made peace with him. He died thinking I hated him."

Finally she understood the burden of guilt he had carried for so long. She couldn't stop herself from reaching out to him. She curved her arm around his neck and laid her palm against his damp cheek. "No, Jason," she whispered. "That isn't true. He knew you loved him. And he was proud of you. Ask Kate and she'll tell you how much." She saw his fingers tighten on the silver frame, and she put her hands over his.

Jason stared at the photograph while the grief and guilt that had weighed on him for years began to ease. It would take time to let go completely, but he knew that Laura was right. The fault was not his—there was no one to blame.

Laura studied the picture along with him. "I want us to keep this on the mantel," she murmured, "for everyone to see. I want it to remind you of the past, and remind you that there is no shame in what he was and what you are."

"Perhaps not to you," he conceded gruffly, "but—"

"It doesn't matter what shallow-minded people think. I fell in love with you because of the man you are. And when we have children, I intend for them to know your family as well as mine. They're going to be proud of their Irish heritage." She smiled unsteadily. "And if you think I can't match your stubbornness, Jason Moran, then you have a thing or two to learn."

He was quiet, his brooding gaze fastened on the photograph, and then he set it aside. "Then we'll keep this damned thing wherever you want it," he muttered. "Hang it on the front door if you like."

A smile of pure gladness broke out over her face, and she knew then that everything would be all right. "Perhaps I will."

Jason pulled Laura into his arms, crushing her to his chest until she could hardly breathe. "I love you," he said hoarsely, burying his face against her hair. "I've always loved you."

"You had a fine way of showing it," she murmured, nuzzling underneath his jaw. "Impatient, sarcastic—"

"Sassy little devil." He let out a long sigh. "I thought if you knew how I felt you'd throw it back in my face. It was safer to let you and everyone else think I wanted you merely as an ornament, a trophy—"

"While I pretended that I married you out of a sense of duty to my family." She laughed softly. "We should have been honest with each other from the beginning."

He rubbed his cheek against her hair, holding her as if he would never let her go. He had never felt such peace. All his life had been directed toward this moment, this woman. The silence was unbroken by anything except the crackle of the fire. Its golden light glinted off the ornaments on the Christmas tree, the glass wings of the angel, the beads on Laura's satin dress.

Laura was suffused with a glow of happiness. She had always loved Christmas, but now more than ever because it was on this night that their marriage was finally beginning, and no greater gift could be given to her. How many holidays he had spent with the Prescotts, always an outsider. But she and Jason would spend a lifetime together and have their own family. And they would make every Christmas as magical as this one. She held him tightly.

"Mo stoir," he whispered, and dragged his mouth from her chin to the valley between her breasts.

Laura recognized the words he had said before. "Tell me what it means," she said, her eyes half-closing as his hand slipped inside her bodice.

"My treasure."

She caressed the back of his neck. "And the other thing you call me—"

"Gradh mo chroidhe . . . love of my heart."

She smiled in pleasure. "Is that what I am?"

"That's what you've always been," he said, and lowered his mouth to hers.

LISA KLEYPAS is the author of twenty-two historical romance novels that have been published in twelve languages. In 1985, she was named Miss Massachusetts and competed in the Miss America pageant in Atlantic City. After graduating from Wellesley College with a political science degree, she published her first novel at age twenty-one. Her books have appeared on bestseller lists such as the *New York Times*, *USA Today*, *Publishers Weekly*, and WaldenBooks. Lisa is married and has two children.

If you loved
<u>*Scandal in Spring,*</u>
you won't want to miss
any of Lisa Kleypas's
unforgettably romantic stories
of four American heiresses
who enter society,
hoping to make a perfect match . . .
and end up finding perfect love.

Now turn the page and enter the world
of the Wallflowers . . .

It all begins with

Secrets of a Summer Night

Available now from Avon Books

Annabelle Peyton is determined to do anything to save her family from financial disaster . . . including marry without love. Her most persistent suitor, Simon Hunt, refuses to offer her the promise of wedlock . . . but he opens the door to a sensuality she has never known. How can she resist?

Following the direction of her gaze, Annabelle saw a dark figure approaching, and she groaned inwardly.

The intruder was Mr. Simon Hunt—a man whom none of them wanted anything to do with—and with good reason.

"Parenthetically," Annabelle said in a low voice, "my ideal husband would be the exact opposite of Mr. Hunt."

"What a surprise," Lillian murmured sardonically, for they all shared the sentiment.

One could forgive a man for being a climber, if he possessed a sufficient quantity of gentlemanly grace. However, Simon Hunt did not. There was no making polite conversation with a man who always said exactly what he thought, no matter how unflattering or objectionable his opinions.

Perhaps one might call Mr. Hunt good-looking. Annabelle supposed that some women might find his robust masculinity appealing—even she had to admit that there was something compelling about the sight of all that bridled power contained in a crisp formal scheme of black-and-white evening clothes. However, Simon Hunt's arguable attractions were completely overridden by the churlishness of his character. There was no sensitive aspect to his nature, no idealism or appreciation of elegance . . . he was all pounds and pence, all selfish, grasping calculation. Any other man in his situation would have had the decency to be embarrassed by his own lack of refinement—but Hunt had apparently decided to make a virtue of it. He loved to mock the rituals and graces of aristocratic civility, his cold black eyes glittering with amusement—as if he were laughing at them all.

To Annabelle's relief, Hunt had never indicated by word or gesture that he remembered that long-ago day at the panorama show when he had stolen a kiss from her in the darkness. As time had passed, she had even half convinced herself that she had imagined the whole thing. In retrospect, it didn't seem real, especially her own fervid response to an audacious stranger.

No doubt many people shared Annabelle's dislike of Simon Hunt, but to the dismay of London's upper tiers, he was there to stay. In the past few years he had become incomparably rich, having acquired majority interests in companies that manufactured agricultural equipment, ships, and locomotive engines. Despite Hunt's coarseness, he was invited to upper-class parties because he was simply too wealthy to be ignored. Hunt personified the threat that industrial enterprise posed to the British aristocracy's centuries-old entrenchment in estate farming. Therefore, the peerage regarded him with concealed hostility even as they unwillingly allowed him access to their hallowed social circles. Worse still, Hunt made no pretense at humility, but instead seemed to enjoy forcing his way into places where he wasn't wanted.

On the few occasions they had met since that day at the panorama, Annabelle had treated Simon Hunt coldly, dismissing any attempts at conversation and refusing his every invitation to dance. He always seemed amused by her disdain and stared at her with a bold appraisal that made the hairs on the back of her neck rise. She hoped that someday he would abandon all interest in her, but for the time being he remained annoyingly persistent.

Annabelle sensed the other wallflowers' relief as Hunt ignored them and turned his attention exclusively to her. "Miss Peyton," he said. His obsidian gaze seemed to miss nothing; the carefully mended sleeves of her gown, the fact that she had used a spray of pink rosebuds to conceal the frayed edge of her bodice, the paste pearls dangling from her ears. Annabelle faced him with an expression of cool defiance. The air between them seemed charged with a sense of push-and-pull, of elemental challenge, and Annabelle felt her nerves jangle unpleasantly at his nearness.

"Good evening, Mr. Hunt."

"Will you favor me with a dance?" he asked without prelude.

"No, thank you."

"Why not?"

"My feet are tired."

One of his dark brows arched. "From doing what? You've been sitting here all evening."

Annabelle held his gaze without blinking. "I have no obligation to explain myself to you, Mr. Hunt."

"One waltz shouldn't be too much for you to manage."

Despite Annabelle's efforts to stay calm, she felt a scowl

tugging at the little muscles of her face. "Mr. Hunt," she said tautly, "has no one ever told you that it isn't polite to try and badger a lady into doing something that she clearly has no desire to do?"

He smiled faintly. "Miss Peyton, if I ever worried about being polite, I'd never get anything I wanted. I merely thought you would enjoy a temporary respite from being a perpetual wallflower. And if this ball follows your usual pattern, my offer to dance is likely the only one you'll get."

"Such charm," Annabelle remarked in a tone of mocking wonder. "Such artful flattery. How could I refuse?"

There was a new alertness in his eyes. "Then you'll dance with me?"

"No," she whispered sharply. "Now go away. Please."

Instead of slinking away in embarrassment at the rebuff, Hunt actually grinned, his teeth flashing white in his tanned face. The smile made him appear piratical. "What is the harm in one dance? I'm a fairly accomplished partner—you may even enjoy it."

"Mr. Hunt," she muttered, in rising exasperation, "the notion of being partnered with you in any way, for any purpose whatsoever, makes my blood run cold."

Leaning closer, Hunt lowered his tone so that no one else could hear. "Very well. But I'll leave you with something to consider, Miss Peyton. There may come a time when you won't have the luxury of turning down an honorable offer from someone like me . . . or even a dishonorable one."

Annabelle's eyes widened, and she felt a flush of outrage spread upward from the neckline of her bodice. Really, it was too much—having to sit against the wall all evening, then be subjected to insults from a man she despised. "Mr. Hunt, you sound like the villain in a very bad play."

That elicited another grin, and he bowed with sardonic politeness before striding away.

Rattled by the encounter, Annabelle stared after him with narrowed eyes.

The other wallflowers breathed a collective sigh of relief at his departure.

Lillian Bowman was the first to speak. "The word 'no' doesn't seem to make much of an impression on him, does it?"

"What was that last thing he said, Annabelle?" Daisy asked curiously. "The thing that made your face turn all red."

Annabelle stared down at the silver cover of her dance card, rubbing her thumb over a tiny spot of tarnish on the corner. "Mr. Hunt implied that someday my situation might become so desperate that I would consider becoming his mistress."

The Wallflowers series continues with

It Happened One Autumn

Available now from Avon Books

Lillian Bowman is beautiful and bold—perhaps too bold for the ballrooms of London society. Her independent American ways are simply not "the thing," and no one makes his displeasure more strongly known than Marcus, Lord Westcliff.

He is one of England's most desirable bachelors, and when he surprisingly sweeps Lillian into his arms, she is powerless to resist him. . . .

Cursing silently, Lillian gave Westcliff a sullen stare. He responded with a sardonic lift of one brow. Although he was clad in a tweed riding coat, his shirt was open at the throat, revealing the strong, sun-browned line of his neck. During their previous encounters, Westcliff had always been impeccably dressed and perfectly groomed. At the moment, however, his thick black hair was wind-tousled, and he was rather in need of a shave. Strangely, the sight of him like this sent a pleasant shiver through Lillian's insides and imparted an unfamiliar weakness to her knees.

Regardless of her dislike, Lillian had to acknowledge that Westcliff was an extremely attractive man. His features were too broad in some places, too sharp in others, but there was a rugged poetry in the structure of his face that made classical handsomeness seem utterly irrelevant. Few men possessed such deeply ingrained virility, a force of character that was too powerful to overlook. He was not only comfortable in his position of authority, he was obviously unable to function in any capacity other than as a leader. As a girl who had always been inclined to throw an egg in the face of authority, Lillian found Westcliff to be an unholy temptation. There had been few moments as satisfying as those when she had managed to annoy him beyond his ability to bear.

Westcliff's assessing gaze slid from her tumbled hair to the uncorseted lines of her figure, not missing the unbound shapes of her breasts. Wondering if he was going to give her a public dressing-down for daring to play rounders with a group of stable boys, Lillian returned his evaluating gaze with one of her own. She tried to look scornful, but that wasn't easy when the sight of Westcliff's lean, athletic body had brought another unnerving quiver to the pit of her stomach. Daisy had been right—it would be difficult, if not impossible, to find a younger man who could rival Westcliff's virile strength.

Still holding Lillian's gaze, Westcliff pushed slowly away from the paddock fence and approached.

Tensing, Lillian held her ground. She was tall for a woman, which made them nearly of a height, but Westcliff still had a good three inches on her, and he outweighed her by at least five stone. Her nerves tingled with awareness as she stared into his eyes, which were a shade of brown so intense that they appeared to be black.

His voice was deep, textured like gravel wrapped in velvet. "You should tuck your elbows in."

Having expected criticism, Lillian was caught off-guard. "What?"

The earl's thick lashes lowered slightly as he glanced

down at the bat that was gripped in her right hand. "Tuck your elbows in. You'll have more control over the bat if you decrease the arc of the swing."

Lillian scowled. "Is there any subject that you're not an expert on?"

A glint of amusement appeared in the earl's dark eyes. He appeared to consider the question thoughtfully. "I can't whistle," he finally said. "And my aim with a trebuchet is poor. Other than that . . ." The earl lifted his hands in a helpless gesture, as if he was at a loss to come up with another activity at which he was less than proficient.

"What's a trebuchet?" Lillian asked. "And what do you mean, you can't whistle? Everyone can whistle."

Westcliff formed his lips into a perfectly round pucker and let out a soundless puff of air. They were standing so close that Lillian felt the soft touch of his breath against her forehead, stirring a few silken filaments of hair that had adhered to her damp skin. She blinked in surprise, her gaze falling to his mouth, and then to the open neck of his shirt, where his bronzed skin looked smooth and very warm.

"See? . . . Nothing. I've tried for years."

Bemused, Lillian thought of advising him to blow harder, and to press the tip of his tongue against the bottom row of his teeth . . . but somehow the thought of uttering a sentence with the word "tongue" in it to Westcliff seemed impossible. Instead she stared at him blankly and jumped a little as he reached out to her shoulders and turned her gently to face Arthur. The boy was standing several yards away with the forgotten rounders ball in his hand, watching the earl with an expression of awe mingled with dread.

Wondering if Westcliff was going to reprimand the

boys for allowing her and Daisy to play, Lillian said uneasily, "Arthur and the others—it wasn't their fault—I made them let us into the game—"

"I don't doubt it," the earl said over her shoulder. "You probably gave them no chance to refuse."

"You're not going to punish them?"

"For playing rounders on their off-time? Hardly." Removing his coat, Westcliff tossed it to the ground. He turned to the catcher, who was hovering nearby, and said, "Jim, be a good lad and help field a few balls."

"Yes, milord!" The boy ran in a flash to the empty space on the west side of the green beyond the sanctuary posts.

"What are you doing?" Lillian asked as Westcliff stood behind her.

"I'm correcting your swing," came his even reply. "Lift the bat, Miss Bowman."

She turned to look at him skeptically, and he smiled, his eyes gleaming with challenge.

"This should be interesting," Lillian muttered. Taking up a batter's stance, she glanced across the field at Daisy, whose face was flushed and eyes over-bright in the effort to suppress a burst of laughter. "My swing is perfectly fine," Lillian grumbled, uncomfortably aware of the earl's body just behind hers. Her eyes widened as she felt his hands slide to her elbows, pushing them into a more compact position. As his husky murmur brushed her ears, her excited nerves seemed to catch fire, and she felt a flush spreading over her face and neck, as well as other body parts that, as far as she knew, there were no names for.

"Spread your feet wider," Westcliff said, "and distribute your weight evenly. Good. Now bring your hands closer to your body. Since the bat is a few inches too long for you, you'll have to choke up on it—"

"I like holding it at the base."

"It's too long for you," he insisted, "which is why you pull your swing just before you hit the ball—"

"I like a long bat," Lillian argued, even as he adjusted her hands on the willow handle. "The longer the better, as a matter of fact."

A distant snicker from one of the stable boys caught her attention, and she glanced at him suspiciously before turning to face Westcliff. His face was expressionless, but there was a glitter of laughter in his eyes. "Why is that amusing?" she asked.

"I have no idea," Westcliff said blandly.

The daring husband-hunting scheme
continues with

Devil in Winter

Available now from Avon Books

*Evangeline Jenner is desperate, so she approaches the most
scandalous man in all of London, Sebastian, Viscount St.
Vincent, with a surprise proposal of marriage. After all,
she knows the viscount will never be faithful . . . so really
how could he ever betray her? And she'll be able to escape
her unscrupulous relatives.*

*But Evie's proposal comes with one condition: no lovemak-
ing after their wedding night. And for Sebastian, that just
means he will have to work harder at his seduction . . . !*

"I'm offering to marry you," she said. "I
want your protection. My father is too ill and weak to help
me, and I will not be a burden to my friends. I believe they
would offer to harbor me, but even then I would always
have to be on guard, fearing that my relations would manage to steal me away and force me to do their will. An
unmarried woman has little recourse, socially or legally.
It isn't f-fair . . . but I can't afford to go tilting at wind-
mills. I need a h-husband. You need a rich wife. And we
are both equally desperate, which leads me to believe that
you will agree to my pr-proposition. If so, then I should
like to leave for Gretna Green tonight. Now. I'm certain
that my relations are already looking for me."

341

The silence was charged and heavy as Sebastian contemplated her with an unfriendly gaze. He didn't trust her. And after the debacle of last week's thwarted abduction, he had no wish to repeat the experience.

Still, she was right about something. Sebastian was indeed desperate. As a multitude of creditors would attest, he was a man who liked to dress well, eat well, live well. The stingy monthly allotment he received from the duke was soon to be cut off, and he hadn't enough funds in his account to last the month. To a man who had no objection to taking the easy way out, this offer was a godsend. If she was truly willing to see it through.

"Not to look a gift horse in the mouth," Sebastian said casually, "but how close is your father to dying? Some people linger for years on their deathbeds. Very bad form, I've always thought, to keep people waiting."

"You won't have to wait for long," came her brittle reply. "I've been told he'll die in a fortnight, perhaps."

"What guarantee do I have that you won't change your mind before we reach Gretna Green? You know what kind of man I am, Miss Jenner. Need I remind you that I tried to abduct and ravish one of your friends last week?"

Evangeline's gaze shot to his. Unlike his own eyes, which were a pale shade of blue, hers were dark sapphire. "Did you try to rape Lillian?" she asked tautly.

"I threatened to."

"Would you have carried out your threat?"

"I don't know. I never have before, but as you said, I am desperate. And while we're on the subject . . . are you proposing a marriage of convenience, or are we to sleep together on occasion?"

Evangeline ignored the question, persisting, "Would you have f-forced yourself on her, or not?"

Sebastian stared at her with patent mockery. "If I say

342

no, Miss Jenner, how would you know if I were lying or not? No. I would not have raped her. Is that the answer you want? Believe it, then, if it makes you feel safer. Now as for my question . . ."

"I will sl-sleep with you once," she said, "to make the marriage legal. Never again after that."

"Lovely," he murmured. "I rarely like to bed a woman more than once. A crashing bore, after the novelty is gone. Besides, I would never be so bourgeois as to lust after my own wife. It implies that one hasn't the means to keep a mistress. Of course, there is the issue of providing me with an heir . . . but as long as you're discreet, I don't expect I'll give a damn whose child it is."

She didn't even blink. "I will want a p-portion of the inheritance to be set aside for me in a trust. A generous one. The interest will be mine alone, and I will spend it as I see fit—without answering to you for my actions."

Sebastian comprehended that she was not dull-witted by any means, though the stammer would cause many to assume otherwise. She was accustomed to being under-estimated, ignored, overlooked . . . and he sensed that she would turn it to her advantage whenever possible. That interested him.

"I'd be a fool to trust you," he said. "You could back out of our agreement at any moment. And you'd be an even greater one to trust me. Because once we're mar-ried, I could play far greater hell with you than your mother's family ever dreamed of doing."

"I would r-rather have it be from someone *I* chose," she returned grimly. "Better you than Eustace."

Sebastian grinned at that. "That doesn't say much for Eustace."

She did not return his smile, only slumped a little in her chair, as if a great tension had left her, and stared at him with dogged resignation. Their gazes held, and Sebastian experienced a strange shock of awareness that went from his head to his toes.

It was nothing new for him to be easily aroused by a woman. He had long ago realized that he was a more physical man than most, and that some women set off sparks in him, ignited his sensuality, to an unusual degree. For some reason this awkward, stammering girl was one of them. He wanted to bed her.

Visions darted from his seething imagination, of her body, the limbs and curves and skin he had not yet seen, the swell of her bottom as he cupped it in his hands. He wanted the scent of her in his nostrils, and on his own skin . . . the drag of her long hair over his throat and chest . . . He wanted to do unspeakable things with her mouth, and with his own.

"It's decided, then," he murmured. "I accept your proposition. There's much more to discuss, of course, but we'll have two days until we reach Gretna Green." He rose from the chair and stretched, his smile lingering as he noticed the way her gaze slid quickly over his body. "I'll have the carriage readied and have the valet pack my clothes. We'll leave within the hour. Incidentally, if you decide to back out of our agreement at any time during our journey, I will strangle you."

She shot him a sardonic glance. "You w-wouldn't be so nervous about that if you hadn't tried this with an unwilling victim l-last week."

"Touché. Then we may describe you as a willing victim?"

"An *eager* one," Evangeline said shortly, looking as though she wanted to be off at once.

"My favorite kind," he remarked, and bowed politely before he strode from the library.